STATUESQUE

Ada Rossi

BUTTERDRAGONS
PUBLISHING

Title: Statuesque
Author: Ada Rossi
Copyright © 2022 Butterdragons® Publishing
All Rights Reserved

This is a work of fiction. Names, characters, businesses, places, events, locales, and incidents are either the products of the author's imagination or used in a fictitious manner. Any resemblance to actual persons, living or dead, or actual events is purely coincidental.

No part of this book may be reproduced or used in any manner without the express written permission of the publisher except for the use of brief quotations in a book review. This includes, stored in any retrieval system, or transmitted in any form by any means – electronic, mechanical, photocopy, recording, or otherwise.

Published by Butterdragons® Publishing
https://butterdragons.com

ISBN: 9789493287013 (ebook)
ISBN: 9789493287020 (trade paperback)
ISBN: 9789493287037 (audio book)

Cover Design by: Dazed Designs

Audio book narrated by Rebecca Sharp

Visible yet invisible
Not how I imagined living
But it changed my life

She found me
And transformed me
Through sacrifice and pain

She gave me home
She gave me family
She gave me the life I deserve

Yet not all is black and white
Lines are blurred
And not everything is as it seems

by Helle Gade

Chapter One

Hannah stood as still as a statue. Someone was staring at her.

It was her first private party and she'd hoped to impress. As a performing artist, it was generally good to be stared at, but the intensity of this man's scrutiny unsettled her. She faced a vast floor-to-ceiling window, through which she could see London's lights. She was high enough to feel dizzy if she allowed her eyes to stray to the street below, so she focused on the party behind her. She could catch its action, if not always its meaning, in its reflection on the darkened glass.

She adjusted her gaze and focused her attention. It was unusual for her to see herself while she was performing. She observed her current positioning, checked her alignment, and made sure no movement was visible. She was trying out her new performance, with an edgier, sexier look. As Hannah contemplated her next move, she wondered whether it was the starer or the party that had sparked her nerves. She was attracting attention she wasn't sure she could handle.

Hannah held a six-foot long metal bar above her head. Her arms were wide, her legs close together. The bar balanced upon her palms, her fingers curled upwards. Her dark purple nails, a contrast to the shiny silver bar, twinkling as it caught the light. There were black velvet ribbons tied around her wrists, giving the impression she was tied to the bar, rather than holding it. It looked stylish and convincing, and was meant to be erotic. Apparently, the posture was fulfilling its purpose.

Hannah had been holding the bar above her head for thirty minutes now, and she was approaching her limit. She would soon begin to shake if she didn't move. When she was perfectly poised, she could stay perfectly still, but she felt unsettled by the starer.

She cast her gaze over the glass, across the party towards the starer one last time, but he had gone. She exhaled, grateful that the distraction had ceased. She took a deep, slow breath, and felt herself relax further. Focusing on her breathing, centring her mind and body upon the simple action of staying still. Breathing in, and breathing out. As still as a statue.

"Isn't she adorable? She's a living statue!"

Hannah started at the sound of Emily's voice. She was only a foot or so away from Hannah's podium, her head level with the back of Hannah's knees. She was inside Hannah's performing space, and the starer was with her. He was still staring, but now he was at close quarters, with his hand on Emily's waist.

Hannah felt under intense scrutiny. Her heart rate increased. A shudder began in her shoulders. She needed to move soon, or risk wobbling under the strain.

"She can contort herself and hold her position for ages. She is incredibly sexy, don't you think?"

Hannah deepened her breath, and transferred her weight forward onto her toes. The invisible shift eased the tension in her calves and prepared her for what came next. She began to bend her back, lowering herself down towards the floor. She had made this transition many times, but hadn't expected to have to do so with such an attentive audience.

"She's moving, excellent, you'll soon see why I adore her so."

As Hannah curved her back she drew the bar downwards as well, the ribbons maintaining the pretence that she was tied to the bar. She kept her arms straight and bowed her knees gently, re-centring her weight as the bar reached waist height. Hannah bent her neck, committing herself to the move, and focused on her landing zone.

She needed to place the bar down and settle her weight onto it before she fell. The bar needed to be placed within a groove upon the stage. It was barely visible, it would not be seen by the crowd. But it was crucial to place the bar accurately, to prevent it rolling under the pressure of her new stance, once she placed her weight upon it.

Missing the spot would be disastrous, and Hannah felt under more scrutiny, and more pressure, than she had believed possible. But while this was Hannah's first private party, it was not her first performance, and she placed the bar perfectly, first time.

"She's new to my troupe, don't you agree she is a marvellous addition?"

Now in a full back bend, Hannah felt the blood return to her hands, and prepared herself for the pins and needles which were about to flood to her currently numb arms.

"So stylish, so unusual, and with so much potential."

Hannah screened Emily from her mind, and placed a lid across her internal awareness of her arms. She reduced the attention she placed on these sensations. It was impossible for most people to understand what she was doing, let alone successfully attempt to do so themselves. But Hannah was well practised at directing her focus as she wished. She considered the control she held over her thoughts to be as critical as the control she exercised over her body. Although, today was testing her limits.

"Highly erotic, of course, I chose her outfit myself."

For the last half an hour, any party guest who was interested in her had been looking at her from the rear. From that perspective, Hannah appeared to be dressed in a body-hugging lace jumpsuit, which was long sleeved but short in the leg, ending mid-thigh. The black lace was actually painted on, with her light skin shining through the lace holes, glittering against the matt black pattern. The effect was to present her as constrained within the costume.

Her front had been visible in the reflection of the window, should any guest have been looking. But without directed lighting, it was muted. Now it was at the forefront of her performance. Bra-less, her breasts swaying, with the body paint barely maintaining her dignity. As the light reflected off the front of her body, bent backwards as she was, the shape of a hand shone from between her breasts. It was upward-facing to the onlooker, downward-facing from her perspective. It sparkled over the painted-on black lace pattern.

"Look at how the light reflects off her breastbone, almost as if she has a thousand sparkly lights laid across her. It's my hand, of course."

Hannah settled her weight evenly across her four limbs, took a deep breath and found the posture becoming easier as she settled into it. She had a further thirty minutes in the back bend if all went to plan. She was determined her first performance would last long enough.

Hannah's new position gave her a close-up look at the starer. Her face was now level with his, albeit she was looking at him upside down. He stood close to Emily, his hand still on her waist, as if he was pulling her in tightly to him. However, the starer was facing Hannah, and so, she found herself examining him.

10

His silver moustache was more perfectly groomed than Hannah's eyebrows. She didn't need to see further than his watch to know she was looking at serious wealth. He had a slight upturn to his lips that Hannah hesitated to identify as a smile, and he sipped his whisky while Emily gripped his other arm. Emily was turned towards him, her eyes on him even as she spoke about Hannah.

"This might be her first party but she's already captured your attention, hasn't she? This performance is designed to awaken your darkest desires, I can see it has worked!"

The starer only nodded, slowly. Hannah could not be sure that he had dark desires, but she sensed his intensity. His eyes did not move from her, he was mesmerised. His gaze was almost as still as hers. Hannah could barely catch her breath, she felt electrified. She kept trying to return to her preferred state of mind for a long-held position; a sense of timelessness and emptiness. She needed to prevent herself reacting physically to her predicament, trapped under the stare coming from beneath the silver eyebrows.

"It is my hand, look, it fits perfectly."

Hannah cringed as Emily stepped closer. She was near enough for Hannah to smell the alcohol on her breath. Emily brought her arm up high above her head, before bringing it down slowly, so slowly, as if to slap Hannah across the breasts. She held her hand just above Hannah's breastbone, in front of the shining shape. It fitted exactly, of course.

"So, you're whoring her out then, Emily?"

Hannah shuddered at the accusation, but her movement was covered by Emily's reaction. She jumped away from the starer with the silver eyebrows as if disgusted with his comment. It was not enough to stop Hannah blushing though.

"Whoring? Of course not!"

Hannah had never been accused of whoring before. Even when she had performed in some of the more decadent streets of London. And yet here, in this private party, she had allowed herself to be dressed this way. She had trusted Emily to know what would work in this environment, in this high-class social world of which Hannah knew nothing.

"It's only whoring if you need the money," said Emily. She seemed indignant at the silver starer's comments, but this was insignificant in comparison to Hannah's horror at her words. Hannah didn't have any money.

Emily finished her champagne and waved the empty glass around to make her point.

"And, of course, Hannah doesn't need any money. She's part of my troupe, she's completely taken care of."

Hannah was no longer feeling so sure.

"If you say so," replied the silver starer, "but try not to over-stretch her, won't you".

There was not a hint of a question mark, and Hannah felt her flush deepen as she allowed herself to contemplate just how powerful this man must be. But Emily had not allowed the silver starer to believe her to be a whore. She had defended Hannah when she was exposed and unable to defend herself. Hannah took some reassurance from that, as if it were a protective blanket from the scrutiny of this starer.

Hannah had so little experience of the world, her ability to differentiate between the wealthy, the powerful and the merely posh was under-developed. Hannah could not possibly know yet, but the silver starer was a rare beast in possession of all three qualities. She could not comprehend power on this scale. She was like a mouse, attempting to determine the difference between a gale and a hurricane. All she felt was the wind. This meant she was inappropriately reassured that the danger had passed.

Had Hannah taken longer to test the strength of the wind, she would have retreated back to her nest to wait out the storm. Had Hannah sensed the hurt the silver starer would usher into her life, she might have reacted differently to his words, words that others may have perceived as a warning. Words that Hannah would later recognise for the weather forecast they were meant to be. A forecast of the coming storm.

Chapter Two

Hannah had finally been left alone, balanced as she was in her back bend, as still as she could be.

With no one immediately in front of her, she had her best view yet of the party. She could see to the far corners of the room from her elevated position on the stage. But this was not a party as Hannah understood parties to be. And not just because she was looking at it upside-down.

For a start, it was remarkably quiet. The current song was a hip hop tune that Hannah couldn't place, but it sounded mainstream and forgettable. She could see corniced ceilings and large bright paintings placed on minimalistic white walls, but no speakers. She could see small but high wooden tables, around which groups of guests congregated to chat, but she couldn't see a DJ. Hannah believed the party would have proven a little dull for the guests, had it not been for the bowls of white powder.

There was a wider age range of guests attending the party than Hannah was used to. At nineteen years old, there was a tendency for everyone to seem old to her, but there were many degrees of age. The silver starer must have been in his fifties, though Hannah thought he looked in fine form, nonetheless. There were many men of a similar age to the silver starer, though none of the women seemed to be.

In fact, she could not see a woman who looked a day older than thirty. Hannah was not sure whether they had all aged extremely well, or whether older women had been eliminated from the guest list in some sort of social cull. Hannah entertained herself for a while musing as to which of these guests were due for the next round of winnowing. From the perspective of nineteen, thirty years of age seemed old.

Emily had placed herself in the centre of the room, and appeared to be in close conversation with two other female guests. They looked remarkably similar to all the others in attendance. Hannah spent a few moments comparing female faces and female forms, all shiny hair and shiny faces, with the vaguely panicked look of the chronically hungry. The powder bowls were popular with the ladies, the plates of food carried by the occasional waiter were less so.

Emily sparkled even here, among others who could be considered her equals in social standing. Her long, dark blonde hair appeared more natural, less bleached. Her face could still express her emotions. Her black jumpsuit was understated, it hung normally upon her frame rather than pinched at the waist to make her look as thin as possible. She seemed like she could breathe. As far as Hannah could tell, all eyes were on Emily. She was the host of the party, after all.

No matter how observant she was, Hannah could not understand how the party worked. Emily was the host although this wasn't her flat, nor were these her guests. Where she excelled was in providing entertainment. Hannah understood that performance artists were the unique selling point of Emily's offering, though she wasn't sure how well Emily was rewarded for their performances. She assumed the catering was outsourced.

Hannah had been surprised that Emily wanted such a static performance from her that evening. Of course, every living statue provided a static performance. But Hannah's established routines involved regular shifts in her position, so there was more activity than many

16

would expect. Movement helped to maintain the illusion of stillness. It acted as its counterweight as well as eased the effort it took to perform. Standing, leaning, squatting; all were easier when they were held for a shorter time, and the contrast between them became more entertaining for her audience.

Yet, Emily's point had been strongly made. This audience was also static. People arrived on time and stayed for the entire party. If she moved frequently, how was anyone to know she was a statue? Thus, Hannah had worked hard to develop an almost motionless routine, incorporating these constrained, long-held positions into a performance of the bonded and laced, of the stretched and curved. Hannah thought Emily's ideas were visionary.

The silver starer aside, she was not certain anyone else was paying much attention to her. This, too, was unnerving for Hannah, as a lack of attention usually meant a lack of funds. At this party, she was not seeking, nor would receive, any donations, tips, contributions, or gifts. Nothing so obvious or vulgar as money changing hands. Not here, not ever. No one was even to know that Hannah used to do that.

****

Hannah had met Emily while she was performing as Cleopatra, one of her favourite statues. It was a busy spring day in Leicester Square, thronging with tourists, and Hannah's performance was being well rewarded. She never performed alone, splitting her takings with her fellow performers. She would feel too vulnerable without them, and besides, it was far more fun this way.

Carly had a superb talent for breakdancing, while Robert was a top-notch juggler. Both of them were full of movement and energy. They performed in brief bursts of activity and then needed a short respite. They complemented each other well, alternating, taking centre stage in turn.

Hannah balanced the trio. She stood over, behind, and in between, as still as a statue for the most part. She could hold the performance space between their individual shows, lengthening their day while allowing the crowds to move along. People only donated once, and it was wise not to let them see how frequently the routines repeated. Theirs was a well-oiled act.

Her Cleopatra was exquisite. Perfect for a sunny day, the weighted linen dipped in plaster cast hung from her shoulders, tightening across her small but pert, unrestrained breasts before falling to the floor. The headdress added inches to her tiny frame, squared across her head and hiding her dark hair.

Hannah's preferred statues always had their hair covered. Hair blew about in the breeze, it added movement even when everything else was at rest. Stillness was an illusion that would only withstand limited interruptions, and a headdress covering her hair helped minimise such distractions.

Hannah altered her version of Cleopatra depending on the supplies she had available. She had applied the base coat of plaster to her body suit, before a sandy-stone coloured overcoat of flour-and-water mix had been tipped over her head. It created the impression she was encrusted within the stone.

It may not have seemed it to an uninformed onlooker, but being a living statue required discipline. The training was intense, requiring cardio fitness as well as strength, and hours of yoga. There were no shortcuts to being able to hold a posture, or to keep still. Stillness required a separation of mind and body, an ability to minimise sensations when needed, and Hannah was good at this. Emotions clouded her focus, and distractions proved de-stabilising.

Hannah was used to being looked at. That was the point of performing. But she'd become acutely aware of a lady watching her. It was unusual for anyone to wait more than a turn or two; this woman had seen Carly's triple backflip three times now, and she alternated her routines. Could she really have been watching for more than two hours?

Hannah's ability to sense time was linked to the physical strain she felt in her positions; when she was in the zone, hours could pass without her noticing. But now she noticed. She noticed this lady's elegance. She noticed her evident wealth. She noticed she had a quality so rare that Hannah could not fail to sense it. Hannah did not know it yet, but this was Emily, and she would change Hannah's life, irrevocably.

Emily had come close to destabilising Hannah's poise, but Hannah was too well practiced to show it. Her returning of Emily's gaze led to a finale of sorts. In between acts, while Carly and Robert were switching, Emily stalked through the crowd. Bending, she placed something in the collection box in front of Hannah, (who later found a card, sized like a business card but with no company name, no address, only 'Emily Woodhouse' and a telephone number).

Emily gave a big wink to Hannah as she rose and said, "Call me."

Hannah had known the moment was sacred. It was pregnant with potential, and Emily had not failed to deliver on that early promise.

Emily's offer was not one of cash but of provision, support, and subsidy. These were important to Hannah but, crucially, she had also offered to sponsor

Hannah into a higher level of society. One in which she would help Hannah to find her perfect match. Hannah hadn't asked how Emily had come by her wealth or her town house in Chelsea, hadn't asked how she earned enough money to support her troupe. She had trusted Emily completely from the first moment they met. Emily said she had her heart set on Hannah joining her troupe. And so, up to this point, Hannah had not looked back.

****

Emily could not have known that her closeness to Hannah, and her discussion with the silver starer, would unsettle Hannah as much as it had. Maybe it was a sign of Emily's trust in her, maybe it was an indication of thoughtlessness. Hannah believed that Emily had her best interests at heart. She had always been true to her word.

Hannah decided that, until she was proven wrong, she would continue to place her trust in Emily, and allow her to guide her through these early steps into this society. And those steps began in a party in a penthouse which was literally, not just metaphorically, a long way up from the streets of London.

20

Chapter Three

Hannah remained upside down, watching carefully for the moment when she could move again.

She didn't have long to wait. The loud clinking of a knife against lead crystal brought everyone's attention towards Emily, who was wearing a look of put-upon impatience which Hannah could see from the other end of the room.

"Folks, may I present.... Xe!"

Emily swung her arm towards a set of double doors which were flung open by two waiters, to reveal flashing lights and loud bangs coming from the room behind. Cheap indoor fireworks. What seemed an obvious trick to Hannah was convincing to the crowd though, who clapped with delight. And through the doorway came Xe.

Xe, pronounced 'zee', was a fire-eater. He was naked from the waist up, and he was lithe, muscular, and supple. He was showing off a chiselled torso which Hannah knew was as painted on as her Cleopatra statue had been. He was Indian by birth and, whether performing or not, he was extremely camp. Hannah had to admit to herself that, in this environment, he looked hot.

"I.... am... Xe!"

Even if he did sound a little daft when he did that. Black leather trousers and boots completed his look, which was simple but eye-catching. Hannah gave Emily full credit for Xe's style. He was not normally so subtle.

Xe held two long unlit torches in one hand, and a lit one in the other, which he placed in a holder about a third of the way into the room. The lights were dimmed,

21

so the flames threw dancing shadows. The effect was dramatic, and Hannah was mesmerised, even from her upside-down position.

Xe lit first one, then the second torch, spreading his legs and holding the torches aloft to form himself into a large cross. He was taking up his performance space. In reaction, some distance formed around him, the crowd curving so they could all see him. These guests behaved no differently than the crowds in the street. And they were spell-bound by Xe.

All eyes had turned away from Hannah, and so, she prepared herself to move. She abided by two rules as a living statue – move when everyone is watching, and move when no one is watching – but she always moved deliberately and with style. In moving, she would be ten minutes ahead of schedule, but as Xe was ten minutes early, she didn't think that would matter too much.

Hannah's next pose was a simpler one, she would find it easier to hold for longer if she needed to. She scanned the crowd, nervous, seeking some contact with Emily, some reassurance that Emily was happy with her performance. But she was too distracted by Xe's antics to notice her. Hannah felt a flicker of jealousy. This helped dispel any remaining concerns she had about moving ahead of her planned schedule.

Hannah splayed her legs a little. Hard for an uninitiated bystander to spot, but sufficient for her to take her full weight into her legs, and be able to lift the bar from its slot on the stage. For the briefest of moments, she feared the magnets wouldn't separate. She lifted off but hung precariously, feeling the familiar terror that her core strength would let her down, but then she was rising, bringing the bar upwards, until it reached waist height. She then began to twist as she drew herself up to her full five feet and five inches.

Hannah gripped the bar to hold it still and level while she spun herself swiftly, moving into her position. Her feet were still facing the window, but now she was twisted at the hips so that the bar was held behind and below her buttocks. She still held it in an open position, facing forward, with both arms square, fronting to the crowd. Velcro ribbons meant the bondage effect was recreated. Hannah still looked tied to the bar.

She could now not only see the crowd, but she could see the guests the right way up. The twisted position felt heavenly after the back bend. She was a little disorientated, as the blood that had flooded to her head now drained away, but nothing she wasn't prepared for. She breathed deeply, centring herself, bringing her focus inward until her body settled into its new position. She refused to be distracted by the spectacle in front of her.

Xe waved his two lit torches around a lot. This was creating the sounds of 'wooh' from the crowd, so they must have made some impact upon them as they flashed past. Hannah was unclear what that impression was. Still, Xe was a performer. She couldn't deny he had style and presence, though perhaps not so much skill as a fire-eater.

The music had changed to suit the routine, a rock tune with a heavy drum beat now played. It matched the drifting smell of burning that interrupted Hannah's deep breathing and caused her to stifle a tickly cough. Guests weren't allowed to smoke cigarettes inside, but Xe was able to smoke them all out, as if they were aggressive bees to be subdued so their honey can be harvested. Hannah speculated to herself, wondering what Xe was seeking to harvest from this crowd.

Xe swallowed the fire from one torch, bringing it away from his mouth extinguished. He then blew fire from his mouth, reigniting the torch and sending a stream of flames towards the nearest table. The 'ooohs' of the crowd became a little more edgy after that, and everyone sidled backwards. Hannah amused herself by pondering how much hairspray was too much hairspray for a party with a performing fire-eater who seemed far too keen to share his flames with his guests.

It appeared she wasn't the only one deliberating upon such deep matters. As Xe repeated his trick towards each of the tables nearest to him in turn, his performing space had grown and the guests were beginning to look a little crowded at her end of the room.

No one was watching her, so Hannah slipped another move in, swapping around her twist. This required her to move swiftly so her feet turned a full circle in a single spin, while leaving her still facing the front but twisting in the other direction. Moving the lower half of her body rather than the top half meant that the bar could stay static, maintaining the illusion of stillness. Hannah's body felt deliciously renewed, as if she had wrung something from her psyche as well as from her spine. She didn't try to hide the smile that crept over her lips; a little upturning would not harm her at this point of the evening.

Xe was gathering himself for his finale, waving his torches around at the guests. Emily appeared anxious, to Hannah's eye, showing a tension in her stance and a fidgeting in her fingers that Hannah had never seen before. Hannah was sure Emily wouldn't let her feelings show if she thought anyone was watching her. It made Hannah wonder just what Xe had in store for his dramatic ending.

The music rose to a crescendo as Xe reached his climax, blowing fire upwards, into the air, a long, exalted breath that continued to erupt long after everyone else had needed to breathe in again. The music and the fire winked out simultaneously, along with every light in the room. It was an impressive effect. The brightness of the final flame was imprinted upon Hannah's eyes. The image remained for a few silent moments, before the main lights began to lift, and the applause began to rise.

Perhaps Xe was not as useless as Hannah had thought. She understood now why Emily was determined to have him perform, despite Hannah's conviction that he lacked a sufficiently wide repertoire to be anything beyond a one trick pony. He entertained the ladies, while remaining available to be matched with the gentlemen. A perfect combination, after all, that's where the real money lies.

"I'm going to call you Mona Lisa."

In her surprise, Hannah could not help but untwist to her side, to look fully upon the silver starer. He had spoken with the gentlest of Scottish twangs, the hint of a boyhood spent far away from the city. He was still holding a tumbler of whiskey in one hand, but he now held a glass of fizz in the other. He looked as if demanding an answer, and, as Hannah's surprise had thrown her position anyway, she moved quickly in an attempt to regain the advantage.

Spinning out of the twist, she moved her feet to stand straight on to the crowd, before dipping down to squat. Back straight, with the bar resting across her knees, it was her planned posture for unplanned circumstances. She could stay here for as long as required, and she remained in character.

She still appeared bonded to the bar, although her breastbone now showed the hand upside down, which – had she thought about it – would not make any sense to a fresh onlooker. But she wasn't thinking about it, because the squat had now brought her to eye level with the silver starer. She didn't look at him, she kept her gaze vague and to the rear of the room.

"You look like the Mona Lisa."

Hannah was going to have to interact some more, it was clear to her that he wouldn't be deterred. His tone was soft but impervious, there would be no digressing from his purpose.

"I'm not sure how you mean. My dark hair?" Hannah felt stupid as soon as she'd said it.

Why am I talking about my hair?

"The smile," he replied.

Of course it was the smile, what else was the Mona Lisa famous for but the smile?

Hannah cursed her lack of discipline for allowing her mask to crack, but she was unable to reduce the turning up of her lips at the sides, no matter how awkward she felt having this conversation.

"Here, surely you are due a break?" He raised the glass towards Hannah. "I'll feel insulted if you don't join me."

Hannah lifted her left arm from the bar, breaking the delicate link within the black velvet ribbons and leaving the bar balanced across her knees as she remained in the squat. Taking the glass, she turned her head to look directly at the silver starer, grinning as she saw he was amused with her.

"Where did Emily find you?"

"I was working just off the West End."

Hannah was not going to admit to being a street performer, not to anyone in this new world she had entered. She would be distraught if anyone found out how lowly her background was, and how poor her beginnings.

"Emily invited me for drinks and made me an offer I couldn't refuse."

She took a sip from the glass, the delicate bubbles an instant indicator of its quality. Hannah, for a moment, was astounded by her new-found ability as a champagne taster. Her first taste had been those first drinks with Emily, only two months previously and now, here she was, judging a champagne's quality on her first sip. It was one more indicator of the changes that had occurred in Hannah's life, ever since her first meeting with Emily. Her first meeting with her destiny.

"Well, make sure she doesn't spoil you." And just like that, he turned and left.

Hannah was not sure what he meant by 'spoil', whether he meant overly pampered, or decomposed. Nonetheless, she recognised his meaning; either would mean her ruin. It was the lightest of warnings yet the deepest of indications to Hannah, that she should realign herself while she still could, before she became committed to her path. And yet, Hannah was still unable to differentiate between winds which blow, and winds which blow you away So she continued to squat there, feeling disappointed that the silver starer had walked away from her again.

The party seemed to have ended with Xe's performance. Two-thirds of the guests had left, and those remaining were in their final throes of farewells. There were many air kisses and waves goodbye, finishing of drinks, and shaking of hands.

The silver starer was deep in conversation with Emily. They were closer to Hannah than the other guests, but far enough away for their discussion to be beyond her hearing. They stood very close together, and they appeared tense. Hannah may not have experienced this type of event before, but she sensed that Emily should be seeing her guests off, not huddled in conversation. And yet huddled is what she appeared to be.

Hannah broke free from the second ribbon and laid the bar in its grooved slot. She straightened her legs, bending over fully with her arms hanging down to the bar.

Bending over with style. Leaving the performance area remained a part of the performance, no matter whether anyone was watching or not. Hannah placed her hands on the stage in front of the bar. Transferring her weight and bringing her legs through the middle, she hopped down the final drop to land on the floor in front of the plinth. Unwatched by anyone, Hannah stood tall for a few moments, before striding across the room, beneath the giant chandelier hanging high in the air and towards the waiters' doors.

"I don't care about the money, you know this, it's about the art. How could you be so callous?"

Emily's voice was elevated in her distress, sufficient for Hannah to catch her words as she paced across the room. But the silver starer hushed her, and so Hannah heard no more.

28

Chapter Four

Hannah was relieved to find herself backstage which, at this party, meant the kitchen.

The waiters were nowhere to be seen, but empty glasses were piled upon one side of the room. Hannah could not see any food anywhere. She shivered, the adrenaline draining from her body, leaving her feeling lightheaded. She was pleased to have escaped from the performance floor without breaking out of her character, and was glad to have maintained her poise for Emily in the face of the silver starer's efforts to disrupt her. However, now she was ready to go to bed.

Xe was washing his hands in a large sink, still in his costume, deconstructing his performance with Katie. She was tall, towering over him. Her bright red hair was shorter than his, her skin lighter, and she was pink across her forehead where she'd caught the sun. Katie was Emily's back-office guru, the person who made sure the right music was playing, or that the bar fitted perfectly within the groove on the stage. She made everything happen, and had a talent for managing the outsourced staff, such as the caterers and the waiters. Hannah had a suspicion that Katie also managed the performers, even if no one ever said so. Emily may be the gracious host of the parties, but Katie was the one who kept the show on the road.

"But I cannot talk to the crowd while the music stays so high, can I?" whined Xe, repeating a complaint even Hannah, in the short time she'd known him, had come to feel exasperated by.

You cannot talk to the crowd because you are exceedingly camp, plus you'll bore them to tears before you've even extinguished your first flame.

Hannah would dearly love to hear Katie's honest reply. Instead, she heard her stock answer, delivered straight, without even a tint of sarcastic hue.

"Emily likes dynamite, and your show is dynamite! Always is, and it's that reliability that is so important to us." Katie passed Xe a tea towel and he began to dry his hands while she continued to reassure him. "She'll find you somewhere to speak, trust me, hun, she's working on it for you. But you know, it wouldn't succeed here, not with this lot. These guests have the attention spans of gnats!"

"Gnats?"

"Never mind, hun. Soon, it'll be soon, I'm sure."

Hannah used to wonder what Xe would say to a crowd if he was given the chance. But she cottoned on quickly that he was not to be encouraged in these thoughts. His show was not destined to be expanded any time soon, regardless of Katie's reassurances. He was simply too dull.

Katie turned to Hannah. "Where's Emily?"

"Still deep in conversation with a guest. Older, silver moustache, Scottish lilt, sexy."

Hannah's slight upturned smile returned as she recalled the way he said 'Mona Lisa' to her. 'Mona Lisa' in Scottish was certainly sexy.

"Ah, Emily's talking to her Daddy, she may be some time then."

Hannah experienced a sense of shock, followed by a moment of clarity. The silver starer was Emily's father? Of course he was! That would explain his dominant tone towards Emily, and how much attention he paid to her performers. Emily hadn't mentioned she had

Scottish roots – like Hannah, she had lived in London all her life. Hannah felt a slight frisson at having thought of Emily's father as sexy. But then, no harm had been caused, and she wasn't about to tell Emily any time soon.

"To the real business then," Katie addressed them both, mock seriousness across her face. "Did you see anyone you liked tonight? Did anyone catch your eye?"

"No," retorted Xe. "There are so few eligible men in London now. It's painful to see how conservative they all were tonight. Some beautiful buttocks, for sure, but tighter than a nun's whaff."

"A nun's chuff, Xe, a nun's chuff," said Katie, "possibly not the ideal phrase to use in the circumstances though."

"How about 'tighter than a gnat's arse'?" quipped Hannah, proud to be thinking quickly. Xe looked even more confused.

"Why not go for 'tighter than a straight man's arse in a gay bar,' then Xe," said Katie, as she kept a straight face that Hannah didn't attempt to match. She openly giggled, pleased to be able to leave her performance mask on the stage and allow her emotions to show on her face again.

"It is all a joke to you both, isn't it! This is my life, you realise, my life!" Xe flounced from the kitchen into the large store-cupboard.

Katie laughed along with Hannah. She pointed at a tray filled with champagne flutes.

"It's already opened, can't see it go to waste. Help yourself."

"Thanks. I think I'll wait 'til I'm changed though." Hannah felt chilled and exposed, now she had ceased performing. She was almost naked in a large cold kitchen, and Xe had locked himself into their makeshift changing room.

"Your bag's behind you."

As Hannah turned, she spotted her tatty rucksack pushed under the counter. Glad to see it but embarrassed by the state of it, she threw on a tracksuit and trainers, not bothering with socks, before bunching her hair under a baseball cap. Performing with it loose had been unusual and mildly irritating, and Hannah let free a sigh as her hair was twisted up and away from her neck.

"Pass me another one of those, will you, hun?" Katie had finished her drink in two large swallows.

"Cheers." Hannah clinked her flute with Katie's just as Emily came flying into the room. Hannah picked one up and handed it to her. She said nothing, downing the champagne in one, and throwing the empty glass against the store cupboard door.

"Oh, come on now," admonished Katie, as Emily began to weep. "How is that going to help anyone?" Katie wandered away, looking through the cupboards for something.

"He is doing it again, he's being horrid to me," squealed Emily.

Hannah placed her hand on Emily's shoulder, her face full of concern. She had not seen Emily so distraught, so disjointed, so discombobulated before. It unnerved Hannah, unsettling her on an evening which had already stretched her beyond her normal operating limits.

"What's happened Emily?" Hannah said, "What did he do?"

"He doesn't trust me to run a successful party, one that makes money I mean, not one that's fun, obviously. They are always fun."

With a start, Hannah realised her rush of concern for Emily meant she loved her. Their time together had been intense, but she only recognised how much her feelings had grown when she saw how upset Emily was, and felt how strongly she needed to make it better for her. Meanwhile, Katie seemed oblivious to Emily's plight and Hannah's response to it, and Xe appeared to be hiding in the cupboard.

"Anyway," Emily continued, "he asked me what you all cost, as if it's any of his business, and he wanted to know how we're all profiting from this. He implied I wasn't capable!"

Emily's voice raced, as if irritated and frustrated. She picked up another glass of champagne, and Hannah braced herself. But Emily drank this one a little slower than the last and held onto it.

"You need to keep Daddy happy, you know, it *is* his money, after all," said Katie, commenting from the rear of the kitchen, from which she had re-appeared carrying a dustpan and brush.

"Fuck no, the fuck it is!" Emily smashed the second flute, throwing it to the floor along with its remaining champagne. Shards flew, catching Hannah's bare ankle. She gasped, from the shock rather than the pain, as she watched Emily lose it completely.

"I have my own money, my own house, it isn't his! My mother left me that house, it's always been intended for me. It's my independence, I'm not owned by anyone!"

Hannah moved in to give Emily a hug, as she continued to shout her justifications.

"He doesn't understand what I do, what we do!" Emily looked straight at Hannah, her eyes wide, a sudden smile upon her face. "You were wonderful tonight, everyone thought so."

"Of course, I always am," answered Xe as he finally came out of the cupboard. He drowned out Hannah's reply. "Darling diva! Dry your eyes, let's get you home."

Walking past Emily, he clapped her on her bum, adding, "Tighter than a nax arse!"

Hannah could not help but smirk at his mangled attempt at the metaphor. Emily, thankfully, took her cue from Hannah, appearing a little mollified, a little flattered, perhaps ready to move on from this episode. Smiling now, she linked arms with Xe and allowed him to walk her towards the door.

"Here, let me help." Hannah lifted chairs out of the way so Katie could sweep up the broken glass. It gave her some cover to think about what she had just seen. She had not realised how fragile Emily was, or how touchy she was about her finances. Something had set her off this evening, even if Hannah wasn't sure exactly what it was.

Logically, thought Hannah, some of Emily's money must be coming from her father. There was too much tension between them for there to be no underlying cause. Did that mean he thought he was owed something by Emily? Did that extend to him feeling he was owed something by her performers? He seemed sure of himself, commanding. Hannah could not imagine disobeying him.

"Emily is often over-excited at parties, she'll be her normal self tomorrow." Katie placed the broken glass in the dustbin and finished her own drink. "Come on, let's not give them an excuse to leave without us, I'm not walking back at this time of night."

Hannah followed her from the kitchen, through the hall, and out past one of the waiters, who had now re-appeared to hold the front door open. Emily was thanking him, full of grace, she had returned to her more elegant self, the person with whom Hannah was more familiar. Xe was holding the lift for them, allowing his impatience to show.

While the lift descended, Emily instigated a group hug. "It was a good party. I'm so glad you joined us Hannah. We are going to have such a good time together!"

As she dropped, Hannah felt a fluttering sensation through her inner ears, giving her the perception of the wind as it blew. She did not appreciate it yet, but she'd had her first real insight into Emily's world. A world of parties with a view over the Thames, of champagne flutes and white powder bowls. It was a world of opportunity and wealth, and one to which Hannah was desperate to feel part. To feel included within, to feel she belonged.

And so, Hannah pressed down on the gentle breeze of anxiety which had been teased into being by Emily's outburst. She did not see that this was also a world of entitlement and dominance, a world of dramas and power plays, a world that she would become desperate to escape from. She did not recognise the evening to be the harbinger of all that would soon follow. That insight only occurred to Hannah much later, by which time it had already come to pass.

Chapter Five

Hannah woke early the following morning, full of optimism for what, she was sure, would be a wonderful day.

She was a natural early riser. She emerged energetic from her slumber as if she was a young child, a trait she had kept throughout her teenage years. She woke refreshed, and ready to go, every day. This had occasionally been a source of consternation for those who shared her bed. No matter how late the night or how heavy the drinking, Hannah was always wide awake first thing. Even after the excitement of her unusual performance the evening before, this morning was no different.

Despite being seven o'clock, the sunlight had yet to penetrate the gloom of her bedroom. Her room was in the basement of Emily's house. Its windows were below street level and so there wasn't much sunlight in the room unless the sun was overhead. There were brighter rooms in Emily's house, but Hannah instantly fell in love with the basement guest suite. She appreciated the small fraction of separation from the rest of the household that the location of the room provided. Her life in the children's home had been full of people, and so that separateness from others had come to be important to her. Space was a precious commodity, as was privacy.

The room was large, covering the full width of the town house and almost half its length. Hannah slept in the double bed closest to the window. There was a second, which was covered in piles of clothes. Some she had worn once and had deemed to be clean enough for a second wear, although not quite clean enough to be returned to the wardrobe. Other clothes laid there, freshly washed but yet to be ironed, and were, therefore, also not ready to be hung in the wardrobe. It was perfectly possible that Hannah had more clothes on the bed than in the sizeable built-in wardrobe covering half of the back wall. The wardrobe's mirrored front reflected her as she began her morning stretches.

She scrutinised herself as she lifted her arms above her head, stretching high, her white cotton pyjama shorts rising as she did so. She leaned first to her left, pulsing further and further into the stretch, and then to her right. She felt the extension it created along the sides of her body, which were sore from the previous evening's twists. Her skin looked distressed from the removal of the paint with a body scrub. Hannah hoped it would create a shine to her skin for that evening, an evening which she was already anticipating with excitement.

She opened the wardrobe door, exposing the numerous outfits hanging within, seeking out her bamboo sportswear. Not a single item belonged to her. Emily loved to shop, and Hannah adored shopping with Emily. She was generous with her gifts, refusing to choose between styles or colours, often buying multiple versions of ensembles which she believed particularly suited Hannah. And Hannah was not one to resist such pleasures. After all, she had an extremely close relationship with her own body. It was the focus of her life, and if she wasn't exercising it, she was displaying it. She was every dresser's dream, and she had quickly become Emily's favourite shopping companion. Hannah's old clothes were buried at the bottom somewhere, and she did not intend for them to surface anytime soon.

Hannah moved on to some leg stretches. She bent from the waist and indulged in a forward fold for a while, hanging her weight from her hips with her knees bent, to allow the spaces in her back to widen through gravity. It felt particularly delicious this morning, as she swung gently from side to side, shaking out the joints in her spine. She wasn't sure how much credence to give some of yoga's ideas about chakras, and toxins. But if twisting the spine did act as a rinse, squeezing out the bad stuff, then the forward fold created the spaces for the good stuff to fill. Or, perhaps, it just felt good. Hannah's hamstrings relaxed and so, she was ready for her run, and ready for the day ahead.

"Morning Freddie," Hannah said, as she poured a glass of water from a bottle in the fridge, and swallowed two caffeine pills. "Won't be a moment, relax, my friend."

She walked across the kitchen, which covered the entire ground floor of the town house. It was not a kitchen like any of those she had seen before she had moved in here, not even on TV. She thought it had more in common with those pictures of offices in Silicon Valley, where bright kids could lounge around on bean bags when they were supposed to be working.

The space was open plan, with double patio doors at the rear. The marble-topped island was sufficiently big to comfortably seat twenty guests, though only half a dozen high stools were currently scattered around it. Kitchen worktops ran along the wall edges, as well as two large fridges, and a professional coffee machine. Hannah felt a little frisson of shame as her eyes caught the coffee machine, something she still underwent every time she looked at it, all these weeks later.

Shaking her head to dispel the unwelcome thoughts, she retrieved her water bottle from the nearest fridge – the liquid fridge, the one in which all the alcohol was kept, chilled, primed, and ready – and grabbed her black leather running pack from the island. Clipping it around her waist was the signal Freddie was waiting for.

"Come on then, Freddie, let's go."

Hannah had never known anyone to be as happy to be with her as Freddie was. He bounded up, bouncing around her, threatening to trip her, and was suddenly extremely excited to be going out with her. She checked her pack's provisions – phone, dog treats, poo bags, keys. She was good to go. She walked past the stairs leading down to her basement room, and then past the stairs leading up to the next floors. No one else was moving about yet. She was the only early riser in the house.

Hannah had learned the hard way that, first, before anything else, Freddie needed to relieve himself. If she didn't plan for this, she would be mid-jog, halfway to the park, and he would be pulling back, crouching uncomfortably on the pavement, casting his eyes downwards.

Freddie was Emily's dog, a pure black spaniel, about three years old, with his fur curling at his ears. He was well trained – Emily had sent him to the best puppy training school for three weeks – but Hannah wasn't sure he had been as well cared for as he might have been. Certainly, he hadn't been getting enough exercise before she moved in. Emily hated picking up after him, and had avoided doing so if she could, and sometimes that meant letting Freddie use the rear courtyard and leaving it for the housekeeper.

Emily had happily delegated Freddie's care to Hannah. She had bonded strongly with him, to the extent that, secretly, she thought of him as her dog now. She spent more time with him, she was sure she cared more for him than anyone else. She loved Freddie, perhaps even more than she loved Emily.

Hannah ran every morning, through the streets of Kensington to the park, around the park and back again. If she couldn't run in the morning, a depression began to descend upon her. Miss one day and she could recover swiftly enough, miss too many and the dark clouds settled in. Sometimes, when she was feeling overwhelmed by how quickly her life had changed since meeting Emily, she remembered her daily runs through London, pounding the same streets as before, which gave her a source of consistency in an otherwise rootless existence. It was the only thing she had brought with her from her old life.

This early on a Saturday was the most peaceful time to be on the High Street. The night owls had receded, there were no school kids or office workers, and the shoppers had yet to swarm. The streets were left to a small handful, lucky enough to see London at its most calm. Dog walkers, joggers, and tramps. Hannah considered herself fortunate to only be two of these three on that fine morning.

Life could have gone either way for her. True, she was pounding through the streets of London, but Kensington High Street was different from the back streets of Camden Town, and in this city, there were as many whose fortunes had deteriorated as there were those who, like Hannah, had found a way to make life better for themselves.

"There are many many different Londons," Hannah commented out loud to Freddie. She often found herself speaking her truest thoughts to the dog, ones she sometimes barely understood herself before articulating them.

Camden Town was edgier than Soho. It had more grime and fewer suburbanites pretending they still had a full night's partying in them, before they gave up and

41

slunk off just after midnight. Regent's Park felt more natural than Hyde Park, more relaxed somehow, less showy. Kensington seemed less 'new money' than Chelsea, possibly unfairly, and Leicester Square provided better crowds than Piccadilly Circus.

There was the tourists' London, the bankers' London, the Westminster bubble and the West End luvvies. There was the socialite world that Hannah had joined. But there was also Dickensian London, still lurking through the cracks in the city, visible to those who cared to look. It was this London from which Hannah had escaped, but she had left others behind when she did so.

Hannah had yet to lengthen her run by adding a turn of Regent's Park, and so she hadn't returned to her old running track yet. She told herself it was too far for Freddie. But in truth, Hannah hadn't returned because she was afraid she would bump into Robert or Carly. She hadn't seen either of them since she'd moved in with Emily, and she wasn't sure she'd be welcome. But until now, she had been too busy getting her new life started to give them much thought.

As she ran, Hannah was hit with a pang of desire to see them again. To see how they looked, and what they were doing. Had their lives changed after she left, or were they carrying on as before? Did she miss them? Did they miss her? Driven by this urge, she turned on a whim, running out of the park and through Sloane Square, heading towards the Thames. Freddie capered alongside her, keeping up, but repeatedly glancing at her. He knew this was not their normal route.

"I know Freddie, I know. Just roll with it." Hannah was talking as much to herself as she was to the hound.

"Let's see what happens. How bad can it be?" She was glad he couldn't answer.

She was heading to Battersea Park, via Chelsea Bridge. It was Saturday morning so she expected Robert and Carly would be training at the outside gym there. She had trained with them for three years, rain or shine, and if their lives hadn't changed after she left, then they would still be there. She wasn't sure what to expect, but as she crossed to the south side of the river she felt her spirits lift, and she picked up her pace a little.

"Let's rock and roll, Freddie."

Chapter Six

Hannah didn't expect to receive a warm welcome. After all, they did not part on good terms.

As she ran onto Chelsea Bridge, her thoughts returned to those final words with Carly, the hurt on Robert's face, and the choice she had been forced to make. It had not been her plan to cut them out of her life completely. She hadn't wanted to fall out with them, but Carly had reacted unreasonably when Hannah told them she was moving out, and Robert's tears had hurt her so much. The combination of anger and sadness had been crippling, and it had stopped Hannah contacting either of them since. She was glad they hadn't wanted her to leave, but they shouldn't have expected her to turn down an opportunity to improve her life, and to move on up in the world.

****

They had lived together in the squat, on a back street off Camden Town, for almost two years. They had shared a room together, they had shared everything together. Robert had found the room through a friend of a friend, another street performer, colleagues tipping each other off to free accommodation, decent performing sites, and – occasionally – some tricks of the trade. This squat was better than most. It was secure enough for the threesome to give up their post-care accommodation; a dingy hostel filled with fellow care-leavers. But a settled squat was hardly a forever home, and Hannah had always expected to leave when somewhere better became available. It had been leaving Robert and Carly behind which had been the problem.

Hannah had met Carly first, on Carly's first day at the care home. Hannah had recently returned from another failed foster placement, and had set her heart against trying for another one. Each time, she worked hard to fit in with the new family, and each time she was rejected from it. The likelihood of a successful adoption became less as she got older, and the rejections became harder to accept, and finally, she lost her faith in it all. Better to square the circle now, than continuing to spin around in the hope of a different outcome. Hannah was ready to try a new approach to finding a family.

Twelve years old and angry at the world, Carly had been a perfect new best friend for Hannah. Carly had a love for dancing and a twenty-a-day smoking habit. She still had a family, she was only supposed to be there for respite care, to wait until it was safe to go home. But Carly never did go home. She stayed angry at the world, but she was fiercely loyal to her friends. Hannah knew she'd made a good choice in pairing up with her as soon as she'd arrived, and she did what it took to keep her friendship.

Carly introduced Hannah to street dancing and, although Hannah was nowhere near as talented as Carly, they competed with each other, driving themselves to ever greater feats, and making endorphins their drug of choice. Fitness became central to both their lives, giving them a feeling of control over something. Carly gave up smoking, Hannah never started. They became inseparable, and would not have believed it was possible for them to love anyone as much as they loved each other. That, however, only lasted until Robert arrived.

Robert arrived at the care home with his arm in a sling and a smile on his face, and had taken a shine to them straight away. He had a slight goofiness about him and a willingness to try anything, irrespective of his broken arm. His first evening had been rather amusing, as Robert attempted to compete with Carly and Hannah, with absolutely no success. Only once he had been truly beaten by them in the dance off, as they laughed at his hopeless attempts, had Robert gathered up their mobile phones, and the small speaker from which music was playing, and threw them in the air, quickly, one after the other. With his good hand, he caught and spun, caught and spun, demonstrating his juggling skills to the oohs and ahhs of Hannah and Carly in equal measure. He was as dedicated to performing as Carly was, and as keen to fit in as Hannah was. And so, Robert made three.

Although they spent all their time together, Robert and Carly quickly became close, thriving from each other's drive to perform. Hannah sensed she was in danger of being cast aside, to suffer rejection again once three became a crowd. To pre-empt this, she instigated 'the pact' and she made Carly swear to it – neither of them would get sexually or romantically involved with Robert. Carly denied having any such intentions, and had always been loyal to Hannah before. But he was a beautiful, dark-brown boy, with a handsome smile he deployed regularly, and Hannah worried that they would succumb, and then they would abandon her. Together, they told Robert of their agreement, and said he could only continue hanging out with them if he agreed to their terms. Laughing hard, he did, and they became each other's family.

Hannah hadn't forgiven herself for creating that damn pact. It swiftly proved unnecessary, when Carly told them she preferred girls. It had never been needed, and yet the pact remained, and still held power over them all. Hannah developed a major crush on Robert. She liked him for a while and, at times, she thought he carried a bit of a flame for her. But she'd driven the pact home strongly in those first few months. Her fear of being left out had made her repeatedly praise the benefits of the three of them together, fighting against the world, being stronger if they didn't have favourites within the group. Her own words had stopped her from getting it on with Robert, no matter how sexy he became as he grew up. And then, she had been rejected from the group anyway. All because she had chosen to work with Emily, and hadn't been able to take them with her.

Although, in truth, Hannah hadn't tried too hard to take them with her. She had been very close to her friends as they grew up, but they were different. Hannah had always known she was different to them, as if she were destined for better things than they were. They might not have understood that, but Emily did. When Hannah had met Emily for that first drink, Emily had handed her a flute of champagne and told her she deserved only the best. It was Hannah's first taste of champagne, but it was not her first sniff of entitlement.

Emily had declared herself star-struck by Hannah's act, not only seeing the power and control it required, but she saw its sensuality too. She described Hannah in increasingly suggestive terms, gazing admiringly at her while topping her glass with the finest fizz. Emily saw the person she really was, and the performer she could grow to be. She had great plans for a living statue performance act, but she had no vacancies for a juggler or a dancer. And her troupe was a full-time occupation, a live-in commitment, after all, there can be no art without allegiance. Therefore, there was no room at Emily's inn for those not performing as part of her troupe.

Hannah tried to persuade Robert and Carly that she was staying at Emily's to ingratiate herself to the benefit of the trio. Carly had made it clear she didn't believe this. She'd been dismissive of Hannah's entreaties, becoming furious and forthright in her condemnation. She'd said some horrid and hateful things to Hannah, as Robert listened, not defending her.

Carly said that she understood Hannah better than Hannah understood herself. Hannah had not got the sense to realise she had been blindsided with lust for Emily's lifestyle. She'd allowed herself to believe that she belonged in those social circles, falling for Emily's promises of easy living. Hannah's hubris had only been enhanced by Emily's attention. Her underlying desires had been long present, but only now were they given the opportunity to emerge. Hannah had been ripe for the picking, said Carly, and Hannah would not forgive her for saying so.

****

Hannah slowed her pace on her approach to the outdoor gym, and began scanning the crowd. Carly and Robert were easy to spot. A circuit class was in full flow, and they were part of a group of six doing burpees, the only two maintaining their speed as the time ticked on. Hannah watched from the path, Freddie panting happily at her feet. She was perhaps fifty feet away, which was close enough to be seen, but not so close as to feel committed. Now she was here, she wasn't sure what she should do.

A whistle blew, and the burpees stopped, and everyone shifted around to the next station. Carly hung back, re-tying her almost-white hair and meandering behind the others. Her gaze strayed in Hannah's direction and she stopped, staring. For a moment, their eyes were locked together. It was too much for Hannah to bear. She lifted her arm to wave to her, just as Carly turned away.

Knowing she'd been seen, and she'd been blanked, made Hannah feel she was about to throw up. She hadn't forgiven Carly but she had made the gesture as a sign of goodwill, and Carly had turned away from her, rejecting her. Pride stopped Hannah from slinking away. She watched them do two minutes of sit-ups, hoping that Robert would give her a better reception. But the whistle blew again, and on they moved to step-ups without either of them glancing her way.

"Sod them, Freddie, let's go," Hannah mumbled as she turned away. "She's clearly still got it in for me, hasn't she?"

As Hannah walked through Chelsea, she spotted the tower in which she had performed the evening before. She paused, but she couldn't work out which window she had been stood in front of. Daylight created privacy for the occupants, but at night, with the light behind her, her silhouette would have been clearly defined for anyone who stood where she did now, and who had cared to look.

That was her new performance space. This was her new world, the society into which Emily had begun to introduce her. Emily had promised her a growing profile on the performing arts scene, as well as finding her a romantic match to help her move up through the ranks. Emily believed that Hannah's unfortunate start in life had artificially knocked her too low on the social ladder, placing her down onto rungs she should not have needed to tread upon. As Emily made clear, and as Hannah felt in her heart, she was returning to her rightful place in the world. She wasn't about to let Carly's pettiness throw her off course.

Near to home now, Hannah searched through her pack for her keys, passed Freddie a treat, and glanced at her phone to see a message from Robert.

Xx

Smiling, Hannah knew he was still there for her, and would continue to be, for as long as needed. She knew exactly how to respond.

XxX

"Nearly there, Freddie, hang in there, we're almost home," sang Hannah at the dog, as she approached her new home, in her new world, reassured that if she needed it, at least one part of her old life was still waiting for her, to help pick her up if it all went wrong.

But, just as the squat could not compare to the pleasures of the Kensington town house, Hannah was certain that, if she gave it some time, and grew into herself a little more, she'd find that her romantic prospects improved in the same way her career prospects had. Emily had introduced her to a world she was determined to make her own. She wasn't ready to settle for a life with Robert, not when so much more had been promised to her.

Chapter Seven

The house was a hive of activity by the time Hannah returned.

Hannah heard the strains of one of the sonatas, each of which she could now recognise from only a few bars. Tom and Lucy were practising, and their music breezed through the open second-floor window. Lucy was a classically trained violinist of international fame. Tom accompanied her, playing on an upright piano, which he often complained was insufficient for someone of his talents. They shared the top floor of the house and they practised all day. They avoided joining in with everyone else and, when there were house parties, there were so many people to talk to that, somehow, Hannah had yet to have a conversation with either of them. In truth, she thought they were rather weird, maybe even slightly unhinged. However, she had grown to love their music. It was heavenly and, even to her untrained ear, she knew Tom and Lucy's performances were exquisite.

Stepping into the house, Hannah let Freddie off his lead and smiled, as he found a previously untapped reservoir of energy, enough for him to go bounding around the island three times, his tail smacking against everyone's legs in turn. Xe let his arms drop and ceased whatever he had been saying to Katie and Emily before Freddie had distracted everyone. Hannah allowed herself a wry smile at Xe's shaking of his head, which he couldn't help but do whenever he was annoyed, but trying to keep quiet about it. He tried to hide his dislike of the dog, but Hannah thought it was blindingly obvious. Emily, somehow, didn't notice, or didn't care.

"You're back later than normal, Hannah, is everything ok?"

Emily may not have been paying attention to Xe's animal interactions, but Hannah beamed to be noticed in this way.

"Yes, all's good, thanks, it's such a lovely day out there, I didn't want to stop running."

Hannah filled Freddie's water bowl as she explained herself, hoping the activity and the movement would help bring this line of questioning to a close. She could maintain her mask and not let her emotions seep through – she would make an exceptional poker player – but she didn't like to lie if she didn't have to, especially to Emily. As Emily had made clear, she could hardly help Hannah achieve the destiny that was due to her if she wasn't open about everything.

"Poor Freddie, you've broken him!"

Hannah glanced quickly at Emily, concerned, but she was smiling, petting Freddie's ears.

"Where have you been Freddie? What have you been up to?"

Hannah squatted to fetch a sachet of dog food from the cupboard under the sink, but no one else was speaking. Emily was directing her question towards Freddie, but obviously he was not going to answer. Hannah was expected to. She couldn't understand her reticence. She had nothing to hide, she had done nothing wrong. The silence dragged on.

"He's getting a bit bored of Hyde Park, I reckon… And the weather is so lovely out there, it is going to be a scorcher today. So, we carried on, we ran south of the river and back."

"Sounds lovely," said Emily. "I thought for a moment you might have been tempted back to your old stomping grounds. You don't miss Regent's Park too much, do you?"

"I mean, the park is lovely, but I've run around it so many times. It's good to explore some other parts of the city, sometimes."

Hannah thought more would be better here, and she tried to make her allegiances clearer.

"Besides, you know, there is nothing more frustrating than bumping into people while you're out running. Trying to make small talk while jogging on the spot only makes people look ridiculous."

It wasn't a lie, exactly, but Hannah could see no benefit that would come from Emily knowing she had been to see Carly and Robert, even if it was only for a moment. Emily seemed satisfied, getting up to refill her glass from the water bottle in the fridge, ice cubes tinkling away. Katie, though, was still looking at Hannah. Hannah made a 'what' face at her, which she acknowledged with a smile. Hannah was not really sure what she meant by it.

"Xe is sharing his reflections on the party last night. Go on, Xe, as you were saying."

Emily returned to the stool, smiling, glass of water in hand, her attention diverted from Hannah's whereabouts and back to Xe's declarations.

"As I was explaining, my performance last night was my best yet. That huge room was simply perfect, I could breathe my fire up to the sky, and across the heads of the guests." Xe became more animated, his voice rising to a crescendo as he declared his desire. "It must be tonight's showstopper. It will be even better in that wonderful space."

"Come now, Xe, you know I would love for you to do that performance every time. But I need to get the best from the entire troupe." Emily waved her glass of water around as she spoke, as if she were conducting an

55

orchestra, her gold watch on her tiny wrist catching the sunlight. "If I was to go with your idea, how would I include the twins?"

"Ah, forget the twins, who cares about those freaks!"

Hannah was shocked to hear Xe being openly dismissive of them. She assumed Emily was fond of them, so to hear him insult them to her face seemed rather discourteous. He hadn't finished yet.

"They aren't trying to make a match, they aren't developing any new material, for sure, why should I organise myself around them?"

"I'm sorry, Xe, but that's just the way it is." Emily's patience sounded stretched. "They are classical musicians, they cannot make minor alterations and create a whole new act like some other performers, each piece takes serious practice. Where there is a grand piano, they perform, and that means they are the central feature of tonight's party. No ifs, no buts."

"No butts, that is exactly the problem," Xe pouted as he complained. "There was not a single eligible prospect for me last night, and what chance tonight, at Arabian Central, of a nice piece of totty turning up?"

"Look, Xe, tonight needs to go as planned. The twins play their set pieces, you come and join them every now and then, eat some fire, move sensually to the music, disappear off and let them play on. It's a marathon tonight for everyone, you, the twins, even Hannah will need to adapt her performance accordingly."

Xe sat heavily onto the stool, pout prominently pronounced. "Okay, so if there is no showstopper, then what about trying out my talk, you know how hard I've been working on it, and I'm sure it's the right time for–"

"Xe, no, not tonight. It is not the right environment for it. I'm sorry, but they simply wouldn't understand you. But I tell you what, why don't you try it out this week, at our party? We'll have plenty of opportunities. And you never know, I may have found a prospect or two for you, and your talk would be a wonderful way of introducing you to them."

Hannah couldn't help but smile as Xe celebrated Emily's offer, his sudden exuberance was contagious. He jumped up and danced around in a tight circle, which revived Freddie, who barked and chased him round trying to jump up at him. That was enough to stop Xe in his tracks. He really did not like Freddie, and as a general rule, Hannah didn't trust anyone who didn't like Freddie.

But Emily had demonstrated her fondness for Xe, making him an offer like that. Hannah had listened to him talk at length about his demonstration, a performance where he talked at length. This was the first time she had heard anyone be anything but dismissive of it. She wondered whether it was linked to Emily's comments about a prospect for Xe, if it would somehow help him complete the match she had lined up.

Hannah had yet to give much thought to the coming mid-week chill-fest. Twice before, she had been to one of Emily's extended mid-week gatherings, which were entertaining for those who didn't need to work the nine to five slog. For a day or two, Emily's house was full of music and laughter, and the promise of sex. A promise which smelt so strongly, it over-powered her.

She had spent the previous parties watching from the side lines, too concerned about making a fool of herself, determined to stay focused on her work, on developing her routines ready for her emergence into society. Hannah had been concentrating on this opening weekend not the midweek party, yet now, it was all Xe could talk about.

"I'll be so impressive, I'll set up at the front here, so the guests can stretch out and relax, and I can spread out over here, in the middle of the room, and no doubt, I'll soon be in the pants of some hottie." Xe had moved away from the island, leaving Freddie being petted by Katie, who had a stronger hold on his collar than Hannah considered to be strictly necessary.

"Okay, Xe, okay, calm down a little, yeah?" Emily sounded indulgent rather than exasperated. "We've still got tonight's star turns to complete, and we'll achieve nothing if we get too distracted. Are you making us all one of those?"

It took Hannah a heartbeat or two to realise that Emily was addressing her. She had started to make her after-run smoothie, and was in the process of adding a second banana.

"Of course, if anyone wants some, shout up, I'm making plenty."

She had been trying to follow Emily's guidance when it came to food, but she found it hard. She accepted that her previous eating and training regime needed to change, and Emily had been kind enough to examine her food habits and make the necessary adjustments to produce a new diet for her.

Gone was the body-building powder Hannah had used since she and Carly had begun competitively training, looking to define their bodies as they built their strength and their agility. Hannah had worked to stay slimmer than Carly – who was hardly large, but was sturdier than some other girls her age – mainly because Hannah liked to use balancing postures in her performance, the more extreme the better, and they were easier to hold when there was less weight involved.

"Go on, you can pour me a small one," said Katie, "Anyone else want some?"

Hannah, started up the blender, rendering any further comment unintelligible. Slimmer's protein powder rather than build-up, water rather than milk or yoghurt, half the frozen berries, a single, smaller banana – if Hannah followed Emily's instructions she would be going straight back to bed after her run, with no energy left to do anything else. Training required the consumption of calories, so Hannah had to adapt Emily's eating plan accordingly.

More calories earlier in the day to fuel her training, and less alcohol and junk food consumed at Emily's encouragement when she decided it was time for them all to have a 'cheat day.' Hannah had ceased weight training and was only using her own body weight as resistance. She had dropped a couple of pounds this way. Her ribs were showing more strongly, her abs were springing from her belly, and Emily had professed she was happy with Hannah's progress.

Hannah was determined to show Emily she was serious about reaching the target she'd been set, and was not going to ruin everything by throwing Emily's eating plan back in her face. She hadn't been concentrating that morning, distracted by Xe's chatter about the party the night before, her post-run hunger, and her anticipation of the parties to come. She knew she would do better in future.

"Cheers, Hannah."

Katie raised the smaller glass before taking a big gulp. She rarely turned down the offer of extra food, and why not? She wasn't a performer, she didn't have to present a particular look, so she could do as she wished, as she often reminded them.

"What about your performance tonight, Hannah, what do you have planned?"

"Oh, I have the most remarkable plan for Hannah tonight. You've been working on those positions we discussed, haven't you? The eagle armed one, and the standing split?"

"Sure, I can hold the arms for thirty minutes without wobbling, no problems. The standing split is really only safe for five minutes, but of course I can rotate through a more neutral, central stance and then split on the other side. So, fifteen minutes in total I should say. And I've some ideas as to how to bring the two positions together, to broaden the routine out."

"Excellent, Hannah. That is exactly what I want you to do tonight. But without body paint this time. I've been tasked with producing a challenging presentation for this evening. Between you and me, I think tonight's host is hoping to shock, to unsettle a guest or two. Maybe there is a big deal due to go down. Who knows? Anyway, who cares? They want challenging, so I've got you an extra special outfit for tonight. You'll need to stay on your feet, though, for the full two-hour performance slot. Can you manage that?"

"Certainly."

"Excellent. Katie will talk you through the details. Xe and I are bobbing out for salads."

Xe returned back to Emily's side at the sound of his name, eager and still grinning broadly. He was more like Freddie than he would like to admit.

"But we will still go shopping this afternoon."

Hannah nodded in agreement, finishing her smoothie as Emily laid out her plans for the day. She hadn't realised she was going shopping with Emily today, but if getting ready for the party was now a matter of an outfit rather than being painted, then there was plenty of time for shopping. And Hannah absolutely adored shopping with Emily.

"We best all crack on then." Emily dismissed her troupe with a final flourish. "It's going to be a fabulous day!"

Chapter Eight

By the time Hannah returned to make coffee, the kitchen was empty.

Hair hanging damply, Hannah wore her pink satin pyjamas. She felt queenly in them. They were not designed for wearing in company, yet they were finished with an eye for quality and detail. They showed how fortunate the wearer was to be treating herself to such luxury for her own pleasure, rather than someone else's.

Freddie had settled into his basket by the back door. Hannah opened it a touch, letting a welcome draft of fresh air into the building, and giving him the opportunity to mooch outside if he was so inclined. The morning sun was now filling the rear courtyard. As wide as the house but only six metres deep, it had been paved some years before, or so the cracks suggested. It contained five statues and a fountain, but no plants.

Hannah could not understand having a garden in which nothing was encouraged to grow. But she loved the statues. The figures of Venetian women, which were nude and mainly without arms, held the sense of grandeur and permanence that sculpture inspired in her. An e-reader and a towel lay abandoned on one of the two deck loungers, which suggested that Katie was not far away.

Hannah could not help but feel a sinking sensation of shame as she approached the coffee machine. It was a true beast of an appliance. Of a professional standard – almost a metre wide, with two grinders – it covered half of the kitchen worksurface. It was sparkling clean and it made the best coffee Hannah had ever tasted. But she didn't think she could ever use it without experiencing a flashback to the horror of her first morning in the house.

****

On her first day, Hannah slept later than she usually did, thrown by the limited light seeping in through the basement window. It took her a few moments to realise where she was, but once she did, she relaxed into the novel sensations of her new home. Fresh sheets, upon a double bed, in a room she didn't have to share, with a private bathroom. Hannah hadn't enjoyed such luxuries before, and she was even more buoyed up because, as Emily told her, she deserved this.

Emily had shown her around the house the evening before, but Hannah could recall very little of that tour by the time she awoke. She had met the twins briefly in the kitchen, poked her head outside to admire the courtyard, and had made firm friends with Freddie. It hadn't taken her long to choose the bedroom she wanted, and she was sure she'd adjust to the limited light in the mornings.

She wasn't intending to go for a run, new to the house as she was, so she headed up to the kitchen in search of breakfast. She petted Freddie for a few minutes, happily, before deciding she was alone and should do as Emily had instructed and make herself at home.

The smell of fresh coffee was mouth-watering as it dripped into the large mug Hannah had placed beneath the left-hand spout. She opened cupboards one by one, finding cocktail glasses, finding dog food, finding the household kitty, and finding miscellaneous attachments to kitchen appliances, which were stuffed below the double oven. She was trying to extract what appeared to be a good blender, when she was interrupted.

64

"I never thought I'd see anyone managing that. You've done it before, haven't you?"

In front of her, hovering at the top of the island, was a woman she was about to learn was Katie, Emily's executive assistant. The person who made everything Emily wanted to happen, happen. Hannah didn't need to know that yet to appreciate that Katie was in charge. She looked sharp and capable, and intimidating. Hannah's heart was beating too fast as she stood there, unsure how to answer, feeling as if she had been caught doing something wrong, but not sure what.

Katie laughed. "All I mean is, it's a professional machine. Normally, I have to show someone three times how to use it before they get it, and yet here you are, grinding yourself a coffee on your first morning here. You must have used this machine before, I assume?"

As Katie's words settled upon Hannah, they spiked a sense of horror at having been caught out, followed by the heat of shame. Of course, Hannah had worked in coffee shops before. She had done any number of jobs, taking opportunities for a little extra cash whenever they presented themselves. This machine was not easy to use without instruction. Only someone who had undertaken such menial employment could have fixed themselves a coffee on their first morning at Emily's house. Hannah had not intended her background to be crystal clear to anyone, and certainly not so soon after her arrival.

"I... I... Hi. I'm Hannah. Pleased to meet you."

"And you. I'm Katie, you are very welcome. And no need to look so mortified, of course you should help yourself to coffee. Emily has never learned to use it, it's great to have someone else willing to."

Hannah's cheeks were burning. She had hoped to be enigmatic about where she'd come from, to follow

Emily's lead in dismissing all talk of the past, and what had brought each of them to where they were. Emily was only interested in the future, in what was going to be, and what Hannah was going to achieve. She had succeeded in convincing her that it wasn't going to matter where she was from. Hannah was quickly catching on to the fact that it would take some concentration on her part if she wasn't going to make more slips like this one, slips that gave her away.

"Emily has told me all about you, it's exciting to have a new performer join us. I was starting to worry Emily wouldn't find someone this side of Christmas! The season starts at the end of summer and it is crazy busy for the rest of the year, so I'm glad you'll be helping us out."

Katie made it sound as if she was lucky to have Hannah there. Hannah hadn't expected this, she'd assumed that everyone would think she was fortunate to be there, and would remind her whenever they had the opportunity. A long history of meeting new housemates had caused Hannah to keep her guard up until she was sure of someone. Katie's easy manner was enticing, but it played in contrast to the astute look in her eye, and Hannah hadn't thought it wise to relax around her just yet.

****

"I'll have one of those as well, hun, seeing as you're brewing."

Katie shocked Hannah back into the present moment – staring at the coffee machine as it fizzled out its final drops of black liquid.

"Sure, no worries, coffee coming up."

Hannah and Katie had bonded over their love for black coffee, good food, and jokes about the other residents. Hannah smiled as she inhaled the fragrant steam from her mug, and watched Katie sip from hers. It was hard for Hannah to recall why she had felt so intimidated when she had first met Katie. She now trusted her, and knew she could be completely open with her.

"So, tonight then, Hannah, are you feeling ready for it?"

"I think so. I mean, I know it will make last night look like a warm up… And last night was more unsettling than I'd thought it'd be. The guests were so similar to each other. It was like being invited to a very large family gathering where everyone has married their cousins."

Katie laughed, a proper head back guffaw, pleasing Hannah. "Oh yes, hun, that definitely sums them up! Inbred cousins is exactly what they all are." Katie caught her breath before continuing, more seriously. "Tonight will be just the same. You turn up, you do your thing, you come backstage afterwards and we get you a drink. Simple. The crowd will be different tonight, though. More global metropolitan elite than upper-middle-class, second-born boys, looking for a little light relief from their futile reality."

Hannah had grown comfortable with Katie's knowledge of her background. She hadn't shared any details, she wouldn't drop her pretence to that degree around anyone. But she could relax, speak her mind, and talk through her concerns. Katie could tip her off, and help keep her from making a fool of herself by doing something without thinking, like brewing up a pot of coffee from a professional standard coffee machine.

"Wow. Big deal tonight then."

"It is. Emily might appear dismissive of the Arabian crowd, but they are ridiculously wealthy. They like the pomp and circumstance of the Royals, and expect everyone to be only one or two steps removed from the Queen. Emily gets that, even if Xe doesn't."

"Oh my, what a way to settle my nerves, Katie. I'm suddenly glad all I need to do is stand still."

"Well, maybe slightly more than that." Katie tapped a small cotton bag that had appeared on the island while Hannah had been showering. "Your outfit is in here, such as it is. And there isn't much of it. Take a look and let me know what you think. But, remember Hannah, you are your own person and you can say no. You can always say no."

Katie's comments jolted Hannah. Only moments before she had been reminiscing about her first meeting with Katie, and now it seemed Katie was referring back to that day too. To an exchange that had stayed with Hannah ever since.

****

"So, new girl, what brings you to Emily's troupe then?"

Hannah had her practised answer to this question ready, but it didn't seem suitable. Katie looked too sharp. She seemed to require a more honest, less voluble response.

"It's a great opportunity. How could I possibly say no?"

Katie's face had darkened immediately. "You can always say no. You must remember that, you can always say no."

"I know, I meant, I didn't want to turn it down, and I'm really excited to be here. Emily is great, and this place is just wonderful, I'm so pleased to be here."

Hannah was gushing, pouring words out without much thought, acting as if Emily's offer was akin to winning the lottery. Which in Hannah's eyes it was, of course, but she didn't have to be open about it. There was something about Katie, though, that meant Hannah found it difficult to pretend otherwise.

"Okay, I understand, fair enough." Katie was relaxing. "It's just… sometimes, some performers let Emily take too many liberties, they don't pay enough attention to their own feelings. It's not unknown for some to come to regret it. Don't be one of those, Hannah. Don't be someone who ends up running away. Speak up for yourself. Don't be afraid to say no if something doesn't feel right."

****

Six weeks on from that early warning and Hannah felt nothing but gratefulness for Emily's guidance and direction. Occasionally though, she had thought about Katie's advice. She wondered who had been here before her, and what had caused them such unhappiness that they had run away. She hadn't asked Katie, but her warning had helped Hannah trust her, and feel that Katie was looking out for her. But Hannah had not felt the need to say no to Emily. Her guidance had always been sound.

Opening the cotton bag, Hannah removed a pile of black gauze. It seemed very light for an outfit. Unwrapping it, she found a bra, knicker and suspender set. Confused, she looked at Katie for an explanation.

"Yes, it is and it isn't what you are thinking. The black underwear is matt and without frills. Deliberately so, because all of it will be on show. Hair down again I'm afraid." Hannah grimaced, but Katie persevered. "I appreciate your thoughts on this, but the look works better with hair down. Try it and you'll see."

"Okay, okay, I'll give it a go. It doesn't actually interfere with my performance, but it's one more thing I have to make sure I'm not distracted by, that's all." Hannah shook out the black gauze. "What's this though?"

"It's a burka. A black gauze, see-through burka… I know… The idea is that you are covered, like many of the Arabian women are, but you are showing what you – and they – are wearing underneath. It's a feminist challenge, and Emily believes the hosts will love it. Apparently, it's a juxtaposition."

Katie held it up against her. It reached the floor, and was wide enough to allow her movement to be unhindered. It would work, but it was not going to leave much to the imagination.

"You don't have to wear it, you know. You can say no."

Hannah heard that warning tone again.

"Well… it's not that different from last night's outfit, is it? I mean, of course I wouldn't dress like this to perform anywhere else, but these are high class parties, aren't they?" Hannah saw an opportunity to test her worry from the evening before. "What we're doing, what Emily is doing… It's art, isn't it? It's not whoring, is it?"

"Oh, hun, no, of course it isn't. It's not a crude exchange of sex for money, it's a performance. People pay for those performances, and sometimes those performances are erotic or titillating. So much so that, sometimes, some of those guests may want to get to know you better. But they don't pay for your time by the hour, do they? Now, this outfit is a little more revealing than last night's, true, but I'm not artistic in the slightest, and I take my steer from Emily. All I care about is that you are clear that you aren't obliged to wear it just because she's suggested it. You can say no."

"It's fine Katie, really. All eyes on me!" She smiled widely, aiming to fake it until she felt it. "I trust Emily, she's the one with the artist's eye, after all."

"True, hun, true. In that case, I'll leave you to get sorted out."

"Katie, wait… Thank you. I do appreciate your concern. And please, put some sun cream on today, yes?"

Katie winked, "Sure, hun."

Chapter Nine

Hannah and Emily were going shopping after lunch.

Whether it was correct to refer to the time of day as after lunch, when there hadn't been any food consumed, Hannah wasn't sure. She squirrelled a banana and a protein bar into her bag in case her appetite picked up. She was fully prepared for that evening's performance, but she was becoming increasingly nervous as the morning progressed. She thought that a walk and a talk with Emily, and some light shopping, would be ideal to settle her down.

"Sorry darling, you aren't coming this time." Freddie's tail was wagging along the floor like a brush, as he sat on his haunches, watching Hannah move around the kitchen island, with a dog treat in her hand. "You are going to stay here with Katie, she'll look after you, alright Freddie?" His tail didn't stop wagging, and the treat was devoured in two chews.

"Talking to the dog again?" said Emily. "I've no idea why you bother. Come on, let's go."

They stepped out into the full glare of the midday sun. Emily arranged a large straw sun hat on her head, so as to ensure a full covering of shade for her face. Hannah hadn't ever seen the midday sun touch her face. Hannah had opted for a neon pink bandana, with her hair twisted up into it and off her shoulders, and a black strapless top. She'd lathered on the sun cream, not wanting to burn, today of all days.

"So, darling, how do you feel about last night?" Emily enthused as they meandered along, heading through the back streets in the general direction of Knightsbridge. "I thought you were spectacular! You drew a lot of attention, you know? Oh, not that I'm about to start spilling the beans, but let me just say, I'm more sure than ever that I'll be able to make a stunning match for you before long."

Hannah was taken aback by Emily's pronouncement. The only person she had noticed paying any attention to her was the silver starer, and Emily could hardly be referring to pairing her up with her own father. Besides, Emily had been so angry with him. There must have been someone else watching her, of whom Hannah had been unaware.

"Well," said Hannah, choosing to answer Emily's first question. "I was very happy with the postures. I mean, they were right out there, at the limit of my endurance, and that was a big thing to try in a new environment. And I pulled it off, so I'm happy about that."

"Excellent. You are right to feel elated, Hannah, it is marvellous to hear you talking positively about it. You were brilliant. Fabulous! When you did that back bend and my sparkling handprint showed on your breasts, I thought it was incredibly erotic, sensual, yes, simply very, very, sexy. We should try to keep that feel for all your performances."

"Yes, certainly, it seems it worked well … Still, the hand was really designed for the back bend. I'm not sure what your thoughts are, but I've been thinking, once I was upright, whether… I don't know really, just whether it lost some of its meaning, I think."

Hannah paused for breath. A breath she then held as she waited for Emily to respond. Emily had turned her head away to look at something across the street, before waving at someone Hannah didn't know. Hannah looked

74

down at her feet, sure Emily was not pleased to hear this implied criticism of her artistic vision. She searched for a way to rectify it, and to end the silence that had descended upon them.

"I mean, in future, I want to make sure I merge the costumes and the routines together more fully... I introduced an error last night, where the routine didn't completely suit the outfit. I don't want that to happen again. At least, that's the standard of the art I'm aiming towards."

"Excellent. That's all anyone is asking of you, Hannah, to work hard and try your best."

It seemed her explanation had been sufficient, and she had been forgiven for her lapse.

"Come, Hannah, let us cross over here. I want to go back to those dresses. I've changed my mind about that long slinky gold one. I'm going to buy it for you this time, I've decided."

Emily had bought Hannah a whole wardrobe full of clothes since she had moved in, dominated by sports gear and lounge wear. Nothing, of course, to match Emily's range of clothes, but she refused to share them. She had not been impressed the one time Hannah had asked. She had taken it as a slur that Hannah wasn't being properly provided for. Hannah had apologised profusely. She hadn't asked again.

Besides, Hannah had not lost the thrill of the conquest, the feeling of elation she felt when she returned home with new clothes. She hadn't worn everything she owned as yet, mainly because when Emily saw something she liked, she bought it in multiple colours. 'Why not?,' she always said, and now, Hannah had been bitten by the consumption bug. They shopped together a couple of times each week, favouring the boutiques of Kensington and Sloane Street, and the department stores of

Knightsbridge. Hannah had not once come home empty-handed.

"Surely you're not worried about tonight, Hannah, not now your first performance is done, and marvellously done, darling."

"Oh no, not at all, not at all," Hannah said, as much to convince herself as Emily, "I wasn't sure what to expect, that's all... But then, tonight may be something else again entirely, so, you know, maybe it'll take a little longer before I'm fully relaxed giving these types of performances."

"No, tonight is not that different, not really. The crowds will change, the balance between power and wealth, fame and fortune will alter, but their desire to be entertained won't. Even posh people are simple creatures at heart, Hannah. Everyone loves looking at young, beautiful men and women, and they want to feel titivated so that they feel sexier themselves. We merely wrap it in a bow and play some music to accompany it."

Hannah was surprised and stumbled, although Emily didn't appear to notice the effect her words were having.

"Still, this doesn't mean we should allow ourselves to get complacent. I think you are coming along well, but we should take another look at your eating plan. I would have preferred to see you drop another few pounds before the season began. Although, in fairness, your abs are looking fabulous! And the line of your calf muscles looks slimmer, so much more beautiful now you've quit the heavy weights. But improvements can always be made, let's not let ourselves get too content, okay."

There was no question in Emily's voice, and Hannah knew there was no response required of her. She

76

was not going to try to explain herself, but she was going to leave the snacks in the bottom of her bag, uneaten.

"Anyway, as importantly, did you see the outfit I've picked for you tonight?" asked Emily. "The see-through burka, isn't it astounding?"

"Sure is, I mean, it is challenging, obviously, because that's the plan, right?"

"It is, Hannah, that's our brief, to be challenging. Our host is less enamoured by the influx of Arabian wealth than many, and although she'll invite everyone along, she is furious at the way they treat their wives. Many have multiple wives, you see, and they don't seem to bring them along to the parties. They're always on the look-out for the next wife, and that is very unsettling to any woman of a certain age, who may be concerned that her own husband is keeping an eye out for a younger model."

Hannah felt rather uncomfortable about the sweeping statements about Arabian men. She worried that it was racist, and portrayed all men as misogynistic and dismissive of their life-partners. And yet, she could not imagine how a culture with multiple wives would be one which any woman would choose, if she had any real say in the matter, or any other viable options. Besides, Emily often talked about groups of party goers as if they were all the same. It was just her way, Hannah was sure she didn't mean to insult anyone.

"The burka though?" asked Hannah, "Is it right to challenge the burka? I mean, aren't we supposed to be for women wearing what they choose, and not being told what to wear by anyone? If they want to wear a burka–"

Emily's laughter interrupted Hannah before she could finish her statement on a woman's right to choose her clothes.

"Oh please, Hannah, please don't be so naïve. How much choice do any of us have? Why wear a top to toe covering to hide yourself if you don't have to? For the same reason we squeeze ourselves into ridiculous high heels. Because we're all looking for someone to love us, and who is going to love us if we don't fulfil their fantasy? So, you'd wear a burka if you were looking to snare a wealthy, conservative Arabian, but if you're after someone a little more contemporary, then flashing your assets is a smarter move. The most important part of making a good match, Hannah, is being clear as to who you are trying to attract. Then, you need to adapt yourself accordingly."

Hannah nodded enthusiastically. She had heard this before and had more experience of it than Emily realised. It was no different to all those families she had tried to fit in with when she was young. Taking advantage of people's expectations of her, being quiet and shy for the first few days to assess what they were looking for in a child – whether they hoped for someone sporty, or overly girly, or smart – and adapting herself accordingly. There were always lots of cues available. The books and toys provided for her were usually clear, even if the clothing wasn't.

Hannah had no reason to doubt that finding a partner would be the same, she only hoped she would be more successful. Emily was the ideal person to help her, to balance the odds a little better in her favour.

"I would like to make a match, or at least have the option to try before too much longer. It's been a while since I even flirted with anyone."

Hannah was worried she was being too forward, too demanding, but she was keen to show her interest. She didn't want to wait. If she left it too long, she would no longer be the new starlet on the block. She would become

78

the also-ran, like the twins, returning year after year to serve up the same performances.

"Well now, Hannah, I don't want to spoil the surprise. But I do have someone in mind for you. Of course, you can always keep yourself entertained, that is what the parties are for, letting off a little steam. But, you never know, this may be a lucky week for you."

Hannah was reassured by Emily's kind thoughtfulness. "Fabulous, thank you. Hopefully we'll spark together perfectly, right from the start."

Emily flirted with the cashier as she bought Hannah the gold dress. Knitted, with sparse sequins around the neckline, it hung beautifully, and Hannah had fallen in love with it as soon as she had seen it, weeks ago. But she'd told Emily she didn't want it. Partly, because she couldn't imagine going anyplace where such a dress would be anything other than ridiculously over the top, and partly, the price tag. Some people spent less buying a car.

Having cast an eye over the party the previous evening, Hannah had overcome her doubts, and realised that a dress like this would be necessary, if she was to move in these circles. And as Emily had made clear, it was well-deserved, it was a reward for her hard work. No one thinks they aren't worth the wages they are paid, and Hannah accepted this was her due reimbursement for the efforts she made. The harder she worked, the more Emily rewarded her. It seemed fair.

Emily bought herself a red, high-necked mid-length dress, gathered around the waist, which flattered her ultra-slim physique. It would look awesome with her big black boots. As Emily chatted while she paid, Hannah found herself pondering where all the money came from. Emily's interaction with her father led Hannah to suspect that she was more reliant on him for finance than she liked to let on. Hannah did not think the party scene could pay enough to keep them in this lifestyle.

Emily carried both bags as they made their way down escalators, exiting into the pedestrianised area to the side of the store. The tourists were hanging around here, watching someone performing in the street. Instinct overtook Hannah, and she paused, interested to see what was happening.

Robert was performing. Hannah's mouth dropped open in surprise. She had never known him to work this part of town. It was a shock to see him now. He was facing away from the store, being filmed by a girl Hannah didn't recognise. She had a big camera, a professional looking one, and was closer to him than Hannah would have expected was necessary. Robert juggled eight rings, which meant that he wasn't trying hard to impress.

"That's a bit cheap, don't you think?"

Hannah jumped. She had forgotten about Emily in her surprise at seeing Robert.

"Lining up like that so the store sign is on camera. I wonder why they're bringing a skill like that, to a place like this? They hardly fit well together."

"True," replied Hannah. "I never thought I'd see him around here. I've no idea, the whole thing seems rather weird to me. What could he be filming for?"

"Oh, who knows, maybe it's one of those gotcha shows, where they string people along for a laugh. I mean, why on earth would you film a juggler?"

"Who knows. Still, he looks pretty good, you've got to admit."

It was out of Hannah's mouth before she'd realised she'd said it. Robert was wearing a one-piece suit, consisting of tight trousers and built-in braces. From her angle, she could see every muscle on his back, glistening in the sunshine, rippling as he threw and caught, caught and threw. It was a look she was more used to seeing on Xe than Robert.

"Hannah, you forget yourself. Have I taught you nothing these last few weeks? You are far better than Robert. You are of superior stock, with better options. You are a performance artist. He is little better than a beggar. He knows his place, and you should know it, too.."

"I know," answered Hannah, quickly, "I didn't mean to suggest that, I meant, I only thought..."

Hannah tailed off, realising that Emily had moved away, stepping through crowds who seemed to melt out of her way. Hannah hurried after her, tracking the over-sized sun hat, but before she left the crowd, she threw one last glance towards Robert.

To find he was looking straight at her. For a fleeting moment, they could have been the only two people there. Hannah felt a rush of feeling towards him, and almost ran over to give him a hug. But she stood, not breathing, as still as if she was performing. Robert smiled at her and winked. She was overwhelmed with relief, followed by delight.

Robert was always going to be there for her. But she was looking for a new life, and that meant keeping her options open for a better match. And so, Hannah turned away from him and hurried across to Emilly, who was throwing the shopping bags into the back of a taxi.

"Excellent, you still want to be with us then, Hannah. For a moment there I thought you wanted to leave."

"Of course not. I was reminiscing for a moment, that's all. I forgot myself." Hannah knew more was needed. "I wouldn't dream of going back. I love what we're doing."

"I wouldn't want to think I was going to all this trouble to find a suitable prospect, only to see you getting the hots for someone like that."

"No, Emily, no way. I'm moving up in the world, just like you said. I'm not going to let anyone hold me back."

Emily smiled, nodding. "See, I knew you were made of better stuff than most people. But you should be careful, one slip and it will all be ruined."

As the taxi eased its way through the late afternoon traffic, Hannah settled her mind for good. She was not going to waste any more of her time thinking of Robert, or Carly for that matter. She had a great opportunity to make the most of herself and her talents. She wasn't about to risk her chance, not for anyone.

Chapter Ten

Alone, Hannah admired herself in the full-length mirror.

Matt black was the ideal colour choice for her underwear. Anything shiny or sparkly would have undermined the clean line of the look. Her pale skin contrasted sharply with her dark coverings, making her appear more naked than the evening before. The fine black gauze was barely visible. It could be a shadow, just a shimmer of a dusty impression. It was so light she could easily have forgotten she was wearing it. These combined to leave Hannah feeling rather exposed.

On a more positive note, she no longer thought she was making fun of the burka, or of the women who wore them. She thought the gauze was too fine to be noticed by any onlooker, and if it was, their first thought was unlikely to be that it was a see-through burka. But the lack of covering meant there was nothing to hide behind. Hannah's hair was loose, dangling around her shoulders. She understood now why Katie had advised her to wear it down. Anything to cover up a little bit more.

Hannah had already tested the movement capabilities of the outfit, so she had run out of excuses. Katie would repeat herself, would say that she could say no, just say no. But that wasn't a viable option this close to the performance. Hannah swallowed down hard on her nerves, and decided that she would roll with it, and trust Emily who, after all, had her best interests at heart.

Hannah began her warming-up stretches, bending and squatting to limber up her lower back and hamstrings. Usually, this was all she required in the way of preparation for a performance. Hannah had a super-flexible spine, and double-jointed hips, and positions which looked extreme to others required little effort from her. She had been able to twist and turn herself into extraordinary positions ever since she was a small child.

Flexible she may have been, but Hannah had no sense of rhythm or timing. She was an awkward dancer. She could memorise some moves, and she could perform well enough by working hard, but there was no spark to her performance, no hook to keep an audience interested. She had not been destined to be a ballerina – or a break-dancer – despite her best efforts.

****

Carly had been kind enough to pretend that she could dance well enough to perform with her, incorporating Hannah into her routines. It had taken Robert's arrival to move their plans forward. Robert was not a dancer, and he was convinced they could each do their own thing and complement each other. This was Hannah's worst nightmare made real; insisting that she decide what it was she wanted to be, and what it was she was good at. She was used to taking her cues from others. She had not defined her own identity before.

For a week or two, she felt lost, and she hovered on the side-lines. She watched the others perform while waiting for some insight to strike her. She was unsettled and feeling increasingly desperate. She managed her anxiety using the breathing techniques her social worker had taught her. She breathed in deeply, expanding her stomach to draw in more air, and then let it out slowly, taking longer to breathe out. Her heart beat slowed, and her thoughts didn't race through her head as quickly. She could reach a trance-like state, where she felt one-step removed from her body.

This was a familiar experience for Hannah. It was a place she often went when she was younger. It functioned as a safe place, somewhere her emotions were under control, and other people seemed a long way away. It was a place she had retreated to less frequently, after first Carly, and then Robert, had become her family.

****

Hannah stopped stretching and reminiscing and stood up straight, looking at her burka-based outfit in the mirror again. She ran through the poses she intended to use at the party, practising them one last time. She checked for niggles in her muscles which may develop into cramps later, and made sure the clothing didn't hinder her positioning. She swooped one arm over the other, twisting until her hands could join together as if in prayer, then lifting them so they were above her head. Eagle arms.

Shaking loose, Hannah stood still with her arms by her side, taking a deep breath which she used to ground herself on her left foot. She drew her right leg up, grasping her ankle in her right hand and stretching her leg out until straight, positioning her foot level with her shoulder. Hannah's muscles were engaged, as she maintained her balance through a push and pull effect between her right arm and right leg, keeping her focus on a single point above the mirror on the wall. The trick to the position was to keep her gaze soft, allowing her peripheral vision to assist her body to make the micro adjustments necessary to keep still. Even after all this practice, she would only be able to hold this stance for five minutes, at most.

Hannah had not intended to pause in place, but seeing her reflection in the mirror, she saw that she was angling her groin towards anyone watching her. The suspenders were of high quality and could stretch with her, but the effect was to frame her groin, drawing the eyes inward, into her most intimate area, which was only covered by a small piece of fabric. The material stretched tight across her labia, and she had to look twice in the mirror to check she was not peeping out.

This directed look upset her balance, and Hannah let go of her pose. She would need to keep her focus that evening. It would be difficult, with strangers looking at her flash her bits in her underwear. She hoped the silver starer wouldn't be there to disturb her concentration again. She needed to minimise the amount of movement she made, as regular changes in position were not in keeping with the aim of her art, or her performing title – Statuesque.

****

It had been Robert who suggested she become a living statue. She hadn't even heard the phrase before he had introduced her to the idea. He noticed how still she could be, and joked that, if she was going to just stand there and stare, she may as well dress up and try to earn a few pennies while she did it. Astonishingly, it worked. The first time she practiced at the edge of the crowd, Hannah realised that all the therapy, the breathing exercises, and the yoga, were finally paying off.

She had found a way to perform alongside Carly and Robert. Together, they built their acts, and Hannah developed her statues. There was Cleopatra, the Venetian goddess, and a reasonable version of the Statue of Liberty. She had been developing her take on Christ the

Redeemer when Emily had shown her how much more she could achieve.

****

Standing still required talent. Emily had been the only person to see that straight away, instinctively understanding what she did and how much effort it required. She saw that Hannah was talented, and she was therefore special and worthy. The mental challenge of stillness, the strength and resilience needed to hold a position without moving. The sense of power she felt when she was Statuesque. Emily had seen that.

In contrast, Hannah had always been sure that Carly and Robert thought she was inferior. Their skills were more obvious than hers, and they designed their show in such a way as to make her performance appear to be a side act, while theirs was the main event. They may have been her family, but that didn't mean they appreciated her. Not like Emily did.

Hannah did not know why Emily could see her talent when Robert and Carly could not. But when Emily had given her that first flute of champagne, Hannah had felt special. Emily continued to make her feel exceptional, in a way which had carried her through any moments of doubt, and through any questions as to why she was leaving the squat and joining Emily's troupe. She was still certain it was the right decision.

It was this belief that convinced Hannah that Emily would successfully match her as she'd promised. It had been unsettling when Emily had first mentioned her intention to partner Hannah with someone from her social world. She was seeking a pairing that would see Hannah soar beyond her beginnings. The primary focus of Emily's performing arts troupe was to move up in the world before she became stale, before she lost her shine, her youth, and her novelty. Before people stopped wanting to look at her.

Hannah had decided that her future was with Emily. She did as she was asked and trusted that, if she worked hard, then she would be taken care of. Emily said she had found a prospective partner for Hannah. She would meet him later this week, and would have her chance to impress. In the meantime, she had this evening's performance to get through. She was determined she wasn't going to let anything interfere with her concentration or her poise tonight.

Hannah threw a cloak around her shoulders, and drew it tight around her waist. She was ready for the party, and thought she was ready for whatever was coming her way.

Chapter Eleven

Hannah was nervous. Her anxiety had been building over the last few days.

First, her poise had been unsettled during her meeting with the silver starer. Then it had been destroyed the evening after, at the Arab party. Now, Emily was hosting a gathering, to which she had invited someone to match-make with Hannah. Knowing this was happening was not helping Hannah to relax, and all her normal methods of calming herself weren't working. She was thankful that Emily appeared not to have noticed.

"Still no sign of Xe, then?" Emily's question startled Hannah from her daydream. "This new performance of his had better be good, he's investing a lot of time in it."

"I'm not sure… He hasn't been very open to feedback, has he?"

Hannah was usually careful not to openly criticise Xe. She was the newest addition to the troupe and, although Xe was bizarre at times, Emily always obliged him. Now, the gathering was approaching and Hannah hadn't laid eyes on him for three days. Not since she had scurried home early from the Arab party, sore in body and bruised in ego. Since she'd moved in, Xe had been a permanent feature in the kitchen. Hannah had never known anyone less able to be on their own than him. And yet, he had locked himself away to develop this new routine. Hannah knew she was not the only person feeling nervous about that evening.

"Ah, not to worry. He'll be entertaining either way!" sang Emily, as she danced around the beanbags.

Hannah was sitting low, at the Moroccan-type table towards the front of the room, around which more bean bags had been scattered, ahead of the party. She was irritable. Her twisted ankle meant she couldn't run, and it was affecting her thought processes. Everything was tinged with negativity. She should have been trying to mask her feelings, and at any other time of her life she would have been. But in her new home, with more space and privacy, she found that no one noticed her mood swings, not in the way others had when they'd lived closer together.

"I'm so excited about tonight," said Emily as she swung her hair behind her right shoulder and draped herself across a bean bag, grinning at Hannah rather inanely. Hannah wasn't daft, she knew Emily was waiting for her to ask – why are you so excited? But Hannah couldn't bring herself to do it. She was feeling grumpy and uncooperative, and less willing to play along with Emily than usual.

"Don't you want to know why?"

Hannah considered Emily's question, and accepted that she absolutely must ask why. Emily's relaxed, spread-eagled form, made her look adorable. Hannah was grouchy because she hadn't left the house since the Arab party, and she was desperate for endorphins. She decided it was time she made some effort to cheer up and be more positive.

"Why are you particularly excited about tonight?"

"I invited Farooq from the Arab party."

Now Hannah's ears pricked up. She had watched Emily spend all night talking with a gorgeous young man. Emily had explained this away by saying that Farooq was fascinated with her performance art, but Hannah wasn't convinced. Besides, other peoples' fascinations didn't explain Emily's willingness to dedicate so much of her time to him. She was an adept social butterfly, she spent time with him because she had a reason to.

"Of course, I haven't invited any of the oldies, I'm keeping the guest list strictly under thirties this time."

Hannah succeeded in not raising an eyebrow.

"Really, I cannot wait to have some relaxed fun, chilling out with beautiful young people. We all need a bit of fun. You haven't forgotten I'm inviting a potential partner for you, have you?"

"Oh no, I definitely haven't! I'm excited!" Hannah could see the triumph in Emily's eyes as she jumped up and down, wary of her twisted ankle, but still excited – incredibly excited, demonstrably excited. This was the reaction Emily wanted, and Hannah didn't feel any desire to thwart her. She didn't need to mask her true feelings, as her enthusiasm was genuine, but nervous tension also rippled through her.

"Oh, Emily, how fantastic, thank you for doing this for me. I'll do my best to impress, I promise."

"I'm sure you won't let me down, Hannah. After all, you are young, stunning, and bendy! Who wouldn't become smitten with you? Besides, I've got a little something to help you along tonight."

Emily reached behind the head of the beanbag she was lying across, drawing Hannah's attention there too. For a moment, she was convinced that Emily was about to taa-daa a large bag of white powder from down there, but instead, she held a small shopping bag.

Emily pulled out something deep red, wine coloured. She held it up in front of Hannah, as if to show off how little there was of it. It didn't seem long enough to be a dress, though somehow, Hannah knew for certain that it would turn out to be. It looked very fine, as if the material was a mere shimmer. Hannah could see that it fell open down the back, and so, it would require going braless. If she was going to wear it, that is. One thing for sure, after the Arab party, whatever dress she wore, she was going to be wearing it bare legged.

"Maybe you should give her some lessons, Emily, we don't want her falling over herself to impress," said Xe, as he sauntered down the stairs, making his entrance with aplomb.

"Excellent, Xe, you have deigned to join us," said Emily. "I'm pleased to see you are still here. I was beginning to wonder."

"Had I known you were missing me, I'd have dashed down here, to be by your side that much sooner." Xe threw himself down onto a bean bag next to Emily. In response, Freddie wandered away from the bean bags and came and sat beside Hannah.

Hannah zoned out as Xe droned on at Emily about his planned performance for that evening. It always had to be about him, there was no point trying to interrupt while he was in full flow.

Besides, she was no longer in the room with them. As soon as her attention had lapsed, her head had returned to the night of the Arab party. She was reliving the whole episode.

****

Hannah threw a black dressing gown over her to travel to the Arab party, to avoid breaching decency laws. Underneath, she wore the black gauze burka and her underwear, which included a suspender belt. Emily had loved the robe, and suggested that Hannah begin her performance wearing it, and take it off for the main show, when everyone had a few drinks in them.

Hannah jumped at the idea, grateful for the extra time she could spend covered up. The event was intimidating. There were more guests than at the party in the penthouse the night before, and they were more diverse. Hannah could see why Emily referred to it as the Arab party. As it was in a hotel, the environment felt more professional and more reserved. With hindsight, Hannah was certain that the daunting atmosphere had played a significant role in de-stabilising her.

The hotel had a sweeping staircase. It rose up, wide, from the middle of the ballroom, before splitting in two, and rising to the upper floor. At the point where the stairs split, there was a plinth. It probably had a stone statue of a lion standing on it normally, at least to Hannah's eye, it appeared to be that sort of hotel. It was here that she was expected to perform.

From the plinth, she could look down into the ballroom, or up onto a gallery, which Katie had told her opened out onto a roof terrace. Tom and Lucy were performing in the ballroom, Hannah could hear their music from where she was stood, but it was not too loud. She could hear herself think. The music settled her, and helped her align her breathing and create the focus she needed for this performance.

Despite her nerves, everything went well for the first hour or so. Her dignity was protected by the cloak. The guests were mingling and drinking champagne. Hannah didn't think they were paying much attention to her. This gave her more confidence, to move her eyes, refocus her gaze, and try to understand the crowd at this party.

The more she looked, the more similar this crowd appeared to the one at the penthouse the night before. She thought she had seen a few familiar faces, though she couldn't be sure. It may have been the popularity of botox amongst attendees at Emily's parties. But she kept an eye out for the silver starer. Only because she needed to protect herself from feeling discombobulated again, of course, she didn't acknowledge any other motivation . On the plinth, high above the crowd, she felt safe, knowing that no one would be able to distract her, or to send her into a spin.

Hannah attracted more attention when she removed her robe. She was, after all, standing still, in her underwear, as the focal point on a majestic staircase. But somehow, the grandness of the building lessened the starkness of her attire. She felt better about wearing the outfit, now she was in her performance space, it looked different than it had in front of her mirror at home. It felt less exploitative, she was pleased to note, when it was placed in its proper context.

Although, as Hannah stood with her arms twisted in front of her, she had to wonder. Was this burka which revealed everything truly a juxtaposition, or was it merely a joke? It might even be seen as insulting. She wasn't convinced anyone at the party understood its meaning, or what it was supposed to be challenging. Good art shouldn't need to explain itself, but that also meant that others could interpret art as they wished to see it, whether this was what the artist intended, or not.

Hannah decided that it was time to move. She untangled her arms, moving deliberately, keeping her head facing forward. As she did so, she sharpened her gaze, bringing her surroundings into view. She could now see the crowd below her, and realised there were more people watching than she had anticipated.

Just in time for my fanny-flashing leg lift!

Hannah breathed deeply, and stood tall, as she enhanced her sense of stillness ahead of the balancing posture. She shifted her weight onto her right leg, breathing in and breathing out, and focused her gaze upon a piece of fretwork in the gallery balustrade. This act of concentration enhanced her peripheral perception, which she needed to prevent her from wobbling. She lifted her left leg up and out, grasped the ankle and assisted it on its way, up towards her head. She took one last deep breath in as she straightened her knee, to place herself in the full, balanced position.

Ping!

Hannah heard the ping as her leg was at its highest and straightest position. It was a terrifying sound. Convinced it was a hamstring, she squealed, and brought her leg down too fast. She leant to the right to counter-balance, looked at the drop from the plinth to the staircase below, and over-corrected, crumbling to the floor to prevent herself going over the edge. She lay there, too scared to move, covered by her own black burka, which wasn't thick enough to hide her shame.

It was the end of her show. Thankfully, the crowd interpreted it as her finale. They politely applauded, and turned their gaze away. Katie helped her limp away, reassuring her that, as far as anyone would ever know, it was all part of the act.

The ping hadn't been her hamstring, for which she remained immensely grateful, her injuries were caused by the topple. She had a twisted ankle and bruised pride. She kept telling herself that it could have been worse, though she wasn't sure she believed it.

Because, it had not been her hamstring which pinged as she straightened her leg to its full length. The noise came from the suspender fastening as it broke, the clasp flying into the crowd. Hannah's flying gusset adornment pinged down the stairs and hit a guest square on the back of the head.

Hannah was mortified when Katie told her. Xe hadn't missed an opportunity to make a joke about it, and Emily had found it marvellously funny. Hannah had not found it amusing in the least, she would hear pings in her dreams for some time to come.

****

"You will wear this red dress this evening, won't you?"

Emily's tone brought Hannah back to her current predicament. Emily wasn't asking, she could tell. But there wasn't much substance to the dress, and she had learnt her lesson about blindly agreeing to Emily's choice of outfit. After all, as Katie kept reminding her, she could say no. However, her discomfort must have shown on her face, as Emily insisted she try the dress on immediately.

"Go on, give Xe and I a spin. Let's see how it looks on you before we make a final decision." Emily was looking at her phone, becoming more excited and eager as she encouraged Hannah to try on the new dress. "Go on, try it on now!"

Hannah wandered off to comply. As she did so, she turned her mind towards the match Emily was making for her, wondering what type of man Emily had chosen. Hannah had dropped a few hints, not too obviously, she thought. She hoped for someone taller than her, and it was important they were athletic, fit, and strong, so she had someone to train with. And hopefully kind, too. She wasn't sure she had mentioned that to Emily, but then, Hannah hadn't seen any need to. She trusted Emily to fill in the gaps and make a good choice for her. She couldn't wait to find out the result.

Chapter Twelve

Hannah was trying to make a decision about the red dress when the doorbell rang.

She was mid-twirl, displaying the backless dress which, she now realised, also swooped low at the front. It was a dress that teased a lot, but was not as revealing as she had first thought. It would not be simple to dismiss this dress, but she couldn't describe herself as properly dressed.

Xe mocked her with his disinterest, whereas Emily loved it. It was her who had spun Hannah around and taken a few photographs, She had insisted she wear it a while longer, convinced that she would love it if she would allow herself to relax into it. Hannah was not so sure. If Katie had been there, she'd be mouthing 'just say no' from behind Emily's back. After Sunday's wardrobe malfunction, Hannah believed she'd be wise to pay more attention to Katie's advice.

As soon as the doorbell rang, Emily bounced across to open the door. Freddie whined at whomever was there, as was his habit. Emily shooed him away, but made poor progress in quietening him, Hannah called Freddie to her, and she squatted to pet him behind his ears. She straightened when she saw Emily's expression. She appeared furious. Hannah could not understand why. She thought Emily should be more grateful that she had calmed Freddie. But as soon as the look had arrived it had disappeared, leaving Hannah unsure if it had been there at all, and Emily was beaming as she opened the door.

"Sally! You made it, welcome, come on in, don't mind the dog, he's being daft. Come on in."

Emily had gripped the arms, and was kissing the cheeks, of someone who looked remarkably similar to her. Both ladies had darker blonde hair, blow-dried into soft waves that showed off their cheekbones to their best advantage. Sally was fully made up, with sharp black eyeliner and red lips, a look Emily preferred when she was in company.

Wow. If I didn't know Emily as well as I do, I think I'd struggle to tell them apart.

Looking closer, Hannah could see that Sally's eyes were darker, and her hair was drier. Everything about her appeared strained. She was further away from her natural appearance than Emily was. She was not quite as thin as Emily, but she was still skinny by any normal standard, and she had dressed to present her physique. Her bare arms showed the muscle of someone who had moulded them into the desired shape.

"It's good to see you Emily, look at you, you look so thin! How are you managing that?"

Hannah felt uneasy as she listened to Sally's extortions of exhilaration. Sally was giddy, as if she'd sunk three gins before coming to the house, but there was also an edge of agitation, lurking beneath her praise. Flattering comments about Emily's thinness created an excuse for Sally to scrutinise her body, and take stock of any changes. Emily greeted her warmly, but she wasn't returning the compliments.

Hannah could hear the sharpness in Sally's voice that sounded posher than Emily's lilt, but which echoed with falseness. Her jewellery was bigger and bolder, and her handbag was more garishly branded. Emily naturally oozed class and refinement. She was make-up and jewellery free, and dressed casually in shorts and a vest, an outfit which would look unremarkable on anyone else.

"Sally, come, meet my troupe."

"Xe!" Xe made sure no one could gazump him and spoil his big reveal, before rolling back to announce, more slowly, "I…am…Xe!"

He stood in the middle of the room, arms stretched out high and wide, in his Xe shape. But it didn't work quite the same when he was wearing a tracksuit. Hannah hid her grin by bending again to pet Freddie, only trusting herself to rise back up when Emily had finished off Xe's introduction to Sally, and she assumed it was her turn.

"And here is Hannah!" exclaimed Emily. "Hannah is my newest performer. Look at her, isn't she stunning? That wine-red colour works perfectly with her light complexion and dark hair, doesn't it? An unusual combination, to naturally be so dark while so light, but Hannah combines it beautifully here, don't you think?"

Hannah looked on, smiling but surprised to be introduced in such a manner. Had Hannah spent more time at horse shows or art galleries she might have recognised the mode of description, but she didn't need to be familiar with those environments to be apprehensive about the turn the conversation had taken.

"She certainly rocks that dress." Sally dropped her eyes to Hannah's legs and took her time returning her gaze upwards. "You are right about the colouring, of course."

"Hannah, give Sally a spin, where are your manners?" Emily laughed as she circled her wrist to indicate to Hannah that she should be turning. "Sorry Sally, I'm still teaching Hannah how to show off her best assets, but her shyness is charming, don't you think?"

"Oh yes, Emily. I'm sure you'll have great success with this beauty. I can tell you have high hopes for her, and with good cause, from what I can see."

Xe didn't try to hide his disgruntlement at the attention Hannah was receiving. It was unlucky that she had been caught flaunting herself in the living room in the middle of the day, wearing the flimsiest of evening wear, but that wasn't her fault. She stuck out her tongue as she twirled round, safely out of anyone else's sight.

"Such pert breasts, have you noticed? She'll be able to go braless like this in company for many years yet." Emily winked at Hannah as she turned back to face them, doing her best to look pleased at the compliments she was attracting.

"Still," continued Emily, "we'll have made our best use of her long before then. I have no doubt we'll achieve great things with her."

Emily picked up the suitcase decorated with leopard print, which Sally had wheeled in behind her and left leaning by the front door. "Travelling light aren't you? Come, I'll show you to your room and you can freshen up."

Hannah watched dumbfounded as Emily walked past the stairs leading up into the house – and towards the empty guest room – and instead carried Sally's suitcase down the stairs into Hannah's basement room. Sally followed close behind her, sounding apologetic.

"I know, I know, but I hate flying with checked luggage. I thought, well, I'm going to see Emily. I assumed we'd spend our time shopping. I can pick up whatever I might need, and see what's hot and fresh on the London scene right now."

"We'll have to clear up a little down here I'm afraid. Hannah might be pretty, but she's not properly house-trained yet."

Hannah's embarrassment deepened. She felt more exposed now than she had done moments before, when she was turning as if on a spit. She should never have assumed she had some privacy. She shouldn't have let her guard down and relaxed, believing it to be her space, and hers alone.

"I'm sorry, I've been spreading out." Hannah gathered armfuls of clothes from the second bed, and smoothed the duvet down.

"So, Sally, you're sharing with Hannah. There's plenty of space down here, bathroom's over there, it should have everything you need."

Hannah dumped clothes on her bed, while Sally tested the mattress on the other. Sally might have been trying to look cross. Her eyes had tightened, although her brow had stayed as smooth as a fully-inflated balloon.

"I hadn't realised you were pushed for space, Emily, I assumed when you asked me to stay—"

"Oh no, Sally, plenty of space, but there's also plenty of guests. Besides, I have no doubt that you and Hannah will get along like a dream!" Emily grinned at Hannah before returning to Sally. "Freshen up, I'll fix us all cocktails!"

Abandoned together, without Emily, a heavy silence descended upon them. Hannah broke free from the weight of it first. She pulled the nearest pair of shorts on, dragged a t-shirt over her head, and shimmied the dress out between the two. She was still braless, but she felt more secure, now she was back in her training gear.

"I'll leave you to sort yourself out, do you need me to get you anything?" Hannah had not had a guest in all the time she had been at Emily's, and although she wasn't sure why she was hosting Sally when there was a perfectly good guest room upstairs, she was determined to be polite.

"There are clean towels in the cupboard below the sink, hopefully everything else is self-explanatory."

Hannah barely waited for Sally's agreement before she turned to make her way upstairs.

Xe mixed cocktails like he was competing to be London's Top Barman, and Emily giggled at his antics. Hannah noted that Xe had re-kindled his spirits as soon as he had returned to being the centre of attention. She was glad, it wouldn't do for him to be fully extinguished.

In preparation for the party, a range of spirits, glasses and accompaniments had been placed along the top end of the island. Xe was mixing Sidecars, Emily's favourite cocktail. Cognac, triple sec, freshly squeezed orange and lemon juice, with a splash of tonic. Emily was convinced it was the high-quality brandy which made the drink as lovely as it was. Hannah thought the sugar from the fruit juice had more to do with it.

"What! Why have you come back up here?" Emily said, as soon as she saw Hannah. "Why aren't you entertaining Sally? And why have you changed? What are you playing at?"

"Well," replied Hannah, taking her time, trying to think of the best thing to say, but realising she only had one thing she could say. "I thought Sally might want some space to freshen up. She's hardly likely to want me watching her take a shower, is she? I've only just met her."

"You never know with Sally, she's always been an exhibitionist. But anyway, that doesn't explain why you're wearing that. The dress looked great! It is the perfect outfit for tonight's party, I must insist you wear it."

Hannah didn't have the heart to disappoint Emily and tell her that the dress made her feel uncomfortable. She hedged instead. "True, but there are still two hours before the party officially starts, and I'm sure if I carried on wearing it, I'd spill something down it." It sounded weak even to Hannah's ears, so she followed up quickly, "I wouldn't be in these scrubs if I was changing party outfits, now would I?"

"I suppose not." Emily appeared mollified, at least she was smiling at Hannah now. "I was worried for a moment that you were going to completely let me down, and just when I've introduced you to such a wonderful prospective match!"

"I… I'm sorry, what?"

Xe laughed so hard he doubled over, as if unable to help himself.

Oh, Xe… Always over-reacting.

"I told you I'd match you well, didn't I?" Emily swept her cocktail glass from the marble-topped island, nodding her thanks in Xe's direction. "Now, concentrate. Sally is a great match. Corporate lawyer in New York, which is dull, perhaps, but well paid. I've known her for many years, and she has made a great life for herself from rather unexciting beginnings. But those connections were good enough for her to make her way in American society. They aren't as attentive to matters of birth as we are, which makes it a perfect place to socially climb, if you're willing to work hard." She raised her glass towards Hannah in a toast. "You two will be perfect together!"

"I… I don't know what to say, Emily… She isn't what I was expecting."

"Come now, Hannah, why isn't she? You were hardly subtle, all those hints you dropped." Emily switched to a mocking tone as she pretended to speak like Hannah. "Training is so important to me, Emily, I would love to be matched with someone I could train with. Don't you think an athletic build is sexy, Emily, I certainly do. Oh, I couldn't possibly fancy someone shorter than me."

Emily shared a look with Xe as she sipped her cocktail. He was laughing so hard he had tears at the corners of his eyes.

"Oh my god, yes, that sounds just like Hannah when she's got one on her." Xe was almost rolling around the floor in mirth.

Emily continued in her own voice. "You whined on and on, but I was listening, and I've delivered. I expected you to be a little more grateful, if I'm honest."

"You're right," Hannah said, choosing her words, "she has many good qualities, as you've pointed out, and I can see the effort you've gone to, in choosing her for me."

Hannah took a deep breath, wondering if there was any other way to put this, before deciding it could only be said the way it was.

"It's just… she's a woman. And I'm not attracted to women. I'm sorry I didn't make that clear."

Hannah was sure she'd been perfectly clear, but she didn't think this was the right time to mention it.

"Oh, I know you aren't gay, but really, when a match is otherwise this perfect, are you really going to let the deal slide away for the want of a dick?"

Xe was crouching down on the floor, crippled by his glee. "Oh, I would. I wouldn't know what to do if I was in charge of the only dick. I'd feel far too lonely."

"I mean… well, I hadn't really given it that much thought." Hannah couldn't see what there was to think about. She wasn't interested in women, she knew that. Carly was gay, Xe was gay, she wasn't. It seemed simple.

"Look, Hannah, let's think for a moment, about what it is we are trying to do here."

Emily handed Hannah a cocktail glass, filled and with a sugared rim, and gestured to a stool next to her. She dropped her voice a little lower as she spoke.

104

"I know you are special, Hannah, and you are destined for greatness. But we don't truly know your pedigree, do we? Therefore, a rising star is ideal for you, don't you see? The social gap won't feel too big, so you won't always be wondering if you are good enough for her. She's a gym bunny, she's ambitious and she earns the sort of money necessary to keep you sparkling, like the diamond you are. Plus, she's got a great flat overlooking Central Park. Are you really going to turn that down because she doesn't have the genitals you prefer?"

Hannah took a deep breath, followed by a second deep breath, while she gathered her thoughts. Emily waited.

She can't be serious? Is this really the match she thinks suits me best?

Hannah took a sip of her drink, which was strong with a sour tang. It was a perfect Sidecar. She didn't want to let Emily down, and she didn't want Emily to think she was not serious about making a match. Emily might not find someone else for her if she turned down the first person she was offered. And, who knows, maybe she would be surprised.

"Is she gay? Sally, I mean."

"Oh yes, one crush after another, trust me, she loves slim women with pert breasts. I'm not daft, Hannah, I wouldn't set you up with someone if I didn't think they could be won over by your charms. And that dress was the perfect way to introduce them, what serendipity that you were wearing it just as she arrived!"

Hannah took a longer slurp of the cocktail before answering. "You're right. I was surprised, that's all. I'll do my best to seduce her at the party. Let's see how well we spark together. I may be pleasantly surprised."

"Oh my," said Xe, picking himself off the floor and taking hold of his own cocktail glass. "Let's drink to that, girl!" He clinked glasses with Hannah. "Down the hatch, my darling, we are going to have so much fun!"

She drained her glass while Xe and Emily were still clinking theirs. Hannah was not certain what the next couple of days would have in store for her, but she couldn't deny, she was eager to find out.

Chapter Thirteen

After her fourth Sidecar, Hannah began to think it was time they ate.

"Excuse me, I'm going to chase up some nibbles. I'm hungry, aren't you hungry?" Hannah probed Sally, hoping against hope that she wasn't one of these women who never seemed to eat anything. Hannah was starving, and was approaching the point of surreptitiously ordering a pizza and sneaking away, taking Freddie for a walk as her cover.

"Sure," Sally shrugged. "I only eat plant-based though, and no carbs, naturally. But yes, some sustenance before any more cocktails would be wise."

"Great, let me sort that for you," Hannah gushed as she rose, only wobbling slightly, which she was sure Sally wouldn't notice. "I won't be long."

"Don't rush, dear," Sally sighed. "There's no reason to hurry back."

Hannah left her sitting low at the Moroccan table, her legs stretched out in front of her, propped upright by the cushions. She continued her conversation with the two other men lounging around the mosaic table. They were a gorgeous pair. One white, one black, both of them strong, both of them tasty. Sexual tension crackled around them. Hannah was sure they could spark an orgy if they were inclined to.

It was painfully apparent to her that she was not crackling that evening, nor was she sparking anything. It was not for want of trying. She was wearing her red dress, she had drunk some cocktails, and she was trying her best moves on Sally. But the promise of sex was not in the air, at least not when Hannah was involved. She desperately wanted to please Emily, and she wouldn't achieve that if she couldn't find a way to entice Sally.

"Katie, where's the food? Tell me there's food!" Hannah's shoulders slumped as she continued. "Plant-based, without carbs, if such a thing exists."

"No idea, hun, but you know there won't be any food until after the joints, so hang in there. In a few hours everyone will have the munchies, we'll order a takeaway, and it'll have been worth the wait."

"A few hours? Can't I crack the weed box out now?"

"Not yet, Emily wants to wait until they start performing." Katie nodded towards two grungy men near the back door, one fiddling with a guitar. "Apparently they only do ballads. We're going to need a little help to slow down and chill out. Anyway, once they're done you can have all the food you want."

"Oh, no, Katie, it's not for me." The angle of Katie's eyebrows showed she knew Hannah was lying, but her smirk made it safe to continue. "It's Sally, she's jet-lagged, she's almost fainting. Surely we have a little something that could pep her up?"

"Well, okay, as Sally needs it. Although carrots and humous is the best I can do."

"Is it low-carb humous? Is there such a thing?"

Katie's smirk broadened. "Tell her it is, there, now it's a thing."

Katie opened the fridge and brought out a plate covered in carrot batons, with a small glass ramekin at its centre, half full with humous.

"Wow, you really are ace, aren't you," said Hannah, pulling Katie into an awkward side hug, reaching to take the plate from her before she could change her mind. "You think of everything."

"Go on now, and slow down on the drinking, Hannah. We've a long night ahead."

For a moment, Hannah was overwhelmed by feelings of love, for the care she'd been shown by Katie. She was almost mother-like, or perhaps her behaviour was more becoming of an older sister or an aunt. Hannah knew for certain that her family was no longer Robert and Carly. It was Katie and Emily who looked out for her, and kept her safe. And hopefully, Sally was about to become part of that, too.

"Here we go." Hannah placed the carrot tray in the centre of the mosaic circle, where three hungry guests descended upon the meagre helping of humous. "We're waiting for the entertainment to start before there's more food."

Sally merely nodded at her, her head down, reading emails on her phone.

"Are you working?" Hannah asked her. "What's your job like?"

Sally grunted. Hannah had struggled to coax more than a few words at a time, and she was running out of ideas to get her talking.

As Sally leaned in to pick up a carrot, Hannah tried again. "How did you become friends with Emily? You must be good friends to be invited to one of these parties, especially to stay overnight. Surely you must have some great stories about Emily to share?"

It appeared Sally did have some fond memories of meeting Emily, because her face lit up, and she put her phone down, her emails forgotten.

"We were at university together. We were on the same floor in halls, the twelfth floor in a block of sixteen, well, you can imagine the parties we had there." Sally paused to funnel more humous into her mouth.

"I had to study a lot more than Emily, of course, law being a more serious subject than art. She had time to dedicate to being fun, being entertaining. She dazzled everyone. We used to have these floor parties, and she would spend the day decorating the common room, and mixing drinks. Everyone loved Emily, and loved those parties. I cannot believe she's managed to turn it into a career, I certainly didn't think she'd be able to make a living out of it. I mean, I know this was her mum's house and everything but still, not doing too badly, is she?"

"No… I don't think so anyway. I think her father helps a bit, though."

Sally gave her a look she couldn't interpret, but Hannah moved the conversation on rather than stop to question it.

"I have to say, she has a marvellous eye for performance art. I've learned to trust her instincts. Her vision may not always be clear until it's executed, but it's been amazing every time."

"Yes, and of course, she has the connections she needs to get plenty of work. She doesn't have to do the hard graft." Sally's tone had changed dramatically, her mind seemed to have descended into a darker place.

Hannah followed her gaze and saw she was watching Emily. Emily was lying across a beanbag, curled up with Farooq, the Arabian man she had been chatting with all night on Sunday. He was very sexy, like a prince from some erotic fantasy novel. They seemed relaxed together. Emily hadn't introduced him to Hannah yet, and she had been too embarrassed to initiate anything herself, given how horrified the Arabian party had left her.

Hannah changed the subject in an attempt to recover the mood. "Oh, go on, there must be more gossip from your university days. Did she break many hearts?"

"Plenty, too many to count. She still does, I've no doubt. Look at her now, fawning all over that poor boy."

"Oh, don't worry about Farooq, I'm sure he can take care of himself. That's just Emily being Emily, I'm sure."

"Let's find out." Before Hannah could disagree, Sally was pushing past her. Hannah collected their drinks and followed, not at all sure that this was a good idea.

Sally sat down heavily on the beanbag, making her presence felt.

"Hi, Sally, how are you getting on?" Emily sat up straighter, giving Hannah a sideways look as she sat down next to Sally. "Hannah's looking after you, I presume?"

"Oh yes, of course, you have such wonderful taste, Emily. Hannah is simply divine."

Hannah was surprised to hear Sally's praise of her.

Sally continued. "You must tell me sometime where you found her. But first, who is this? I insist you introduce me."

"Why, of course, Sally, this is Farooq. Farooq, this is Sally, a university friend who has flown all the way from New York, especially for my party."

"Oh, a fellow jet-setter, how exciting." Farooq offered his hand to Sally. "I love New York, I've not been for a few months, but I will definitely be back by the fall. I adore the colours in Central Park, it's simply the best time of year to be there. And you must be Hannah, I've heard lots of good things about you."

"Farooq, you are such a charmer! Listen, you entertain Sally for a few moments while Hannah and I fill our glasses. Same again?"

Emily made a beeline for the drinks table, nodding as Hannah began mixing more drinks. "So, how

111

are you getting on with Sally? She seems rather taken with you."

"I'm not sure, really… She speaks highly of me to you, but she doesn't seem that interested in me when you're not around. I'm trying to get her chatting but–"

"Oh, Hannah, she isn't going to be interested in what you have to say!" She laughed as she placed her hand on Hannah's shoulder, squeezing it too hard for her to feel comfortable. "Sally spends all day talking with intelligent people while she is at work, why would you be able to attract her with your chatter? Conversational skills are something you'll have to rely on later in life, when you look over-cooked from all that sunlight you insist upon. While you are supple and lithe, and free from botox and fillers, stick to what you're best at. Charm her in other ways. Alcohol will assist, but make sure she smokes a little too when it's time."

"Okay thanks, that's helpful." Hannah wasn't sure how she'd do this, but the pressure was off her linguistic skills, at least.

Sally was watching them while in conversation with Farooq. Thinking it may be easier to tempt Sally by making eyes across the room, Hannah smiled at her, and scrambled for a reason to delay going back.

"So, what's the crack with Farooq then?" she asked Emily, "I take it he was at the party on Sunday?"

"Yes, I met him there. His father's the Crown Prince of somewhere, I cannot recall where, they blend into one as far as I can tell. But wow, do they have money! He is great marriage material, obviously. He works in the city, unfortunately, he's one of those hedge fund guys, but hey, no one is perfect. And isn't he hot?"

"He sure is, Emily. Do you think he's looking for a bride? You'd make a delightful princess."

"Truly, he doesn't know what he's looking for. He says he's promised to someone back home – it's political, you understand – but they do have multiple wives out there, so who knows how he will choose to organise himself. He looks like he can service more than one, though, doesn't he?"

Hannah and Emily paused to stare at Sally and Farooq, who were gazing back at them. Finally, sexual tension crackled around Hannah. Unfortunately, the spell was swiftly broken.

"I...am... Xe!"

Down the stairs jumped Xe, wearing a leather vest with denim shorts. Everyone stopped talking and turned towards him.

"This had better be good," whispered Emily.

"You know me from my show-stopping performances as a fire-eater, but tonight, I am not going to breathe fire over you. No, tonight, for this special, intimate performance, I'm going to share my joy of mindfulness with you, and guide you through some practices to heal your body and soothe your soul." Xe took a seat on the floor with his legs crossed in front of him. He looked as if he was about to hum.

"Quick, we must get the joints out, no one is going to make it through this without a little help." Emily picked up a wooden box decorated with pink swirls, and pushed it at Hannah, distracting her from Xe's performance. "Here, get going, be swift."

Hannah moved through the back of the crowd, handing out a joint to each guest, placing it down near those who didn't readily accept one. Not the twins – Tom and Lucy only agreed to attend the parties if they could sit quietly at the back – but everyone else was included. At previous parties, every guest had smoked, some more enthusiastically than others.

Hannah had not escaped it. She reassured herself that it didn't count, as she hadn't inhaled the smoke, she had only puffed, elaborately. She had seen what drugs had done to some of the kids in the care home. They were promised an escape from their own private hell, but they were delivered to a new, shared one. Exercise had always been her drug of choice, and she had been adamantly anti-drug for many years.

At least there are no powder bowls! And so, Hannah made her peace with taking a few puffs on a joint, safely insulated by the assurance that there was a worse choice that she could be making, so this option couldn't be that bad.

"Hey, Xe, breathe us a light, yeah?" There was laughter in the crowd, but Xe didn't seem impressed with the interruption. Having left them until last, Hannah returned to Farooq and Sally. Farooq pulled out a lighter, and looked sexy and smooth, as he lit three joints with one sweep of his flame.

Distracted, Hannah took a deep drag. She spluttered, fighting hard to overcome it. She was not the only choker on the first fiery pull. Clearing her eyes, she saw that Farooq was immersed in Xe's performance, barely noticing that Emily had returned. Sally certainly did.

Emily took Farooq's arm and wrapped it around herself, snuggling in, and succeeding in bringing Farooq's attention back to them.

"Isn't he wonderful?" he said.

"You are being sarcastic, I assume?" said Sally, "I've been in the US too long, I can't always tell anymore."

"Oh no, I love him, listen to how powerful he is in his phrasing." Farooq paused to smoke, leaning his head back and blowing three perfect smoke rings, one after the other. They drifted over to the staircases, over Xe's head, who continued his performance, regardless. Farooq hadn't finished complementing him. "It's very different to his fire-eating performance, he's surprisingly versatile."

"Well, Emily does have a knack of turning out performing artists who are very popular, don't you, my darling?" said Sally. "Are you a performer yourself, Farooq? Emily didn't say what you do."

"Sally, really, that is none of your business, why are you questioning my guests?" Emily allowed herself to look cross, more so than Hannah could recall seeing before. "You have Hannah to play with, why are you here, interrupting us?"

Sally rose and paused, looking as if she had a lot to say, before sighing and stalking off towards the kitchen, a glass in one hand, a joint in the other.

"Go, Hannah," said Emily. "Go after her. Now's your chance. Don't mess it up."

Hannah stepped through the back door, taking Freddie with her for moral support. He bounded around the courtyard as she took some deep breaths. Sally was perched on the fountain's edge, smoking furiously.

"Some air seems a good idea," said Hannah as she joined her, sitting closer than she would normally have done. "I think Freddie needed some, anyway. Do you think dogs can get high from second-hand smoke?"

Sally didn't answer, she ran a hand through her hair and held it back from her face, taking a final hurried series of puffs. She turned towards Hannah, throwing the butt into the fountain, where it sizzled. She closed her eyes, her face only inches from Hannah's, and she moaned.

Ignoring the smoky haze, Hannah took the opportunity presented to her, and touched her lips to

Sally's. She felt them slide open to greet her, and Hannah moved in to deepen their kiss.

Sally shoved her away. "What the fuck do you think you're doing?"

Hannah braced herself, narrowly avoiding falling into the fountain.

Sally towered over her. "Do you really think someone like me would be interested in someone like you? Who are you, anyway? One of Emily's whores, that's who."

Hannah's horror grew. Tears sprung as she felt the full force of Sally's disgust with her. She fled, straight through Xe's chanting and breathing session and down into the safety of her basement room.

Following her through the now silent crowd came Sally's final rejection of her.

"I don't want you, you performing pet. Not even for one night."

Chapter Fourteen

The water was almost hot enough to burn Hannah, as she sobbed away her hurt in the shower.

She'd always found the bathroom to be a good place to hide. Locks on the door prevented unwelcome interruptions, and hot water disguised swollen faces and red eyes. When she wanted to let her pain out without anyone noticing, and wanted to take the sting away but still keep her mask on, then the bathroom provided the perfect cover. She hadn't felt the need to do this since moving in with Emily, and it was heart-wrenching to need to do it now.

Hannah shouldn't have worried. No one followed her downstairs to check if she was okay. The party continued on without her. Xe finished his performance to a round of applause, surprisingly, and a guitarist started strumming a slow song. Hannah's mood sank lower as melancholy lyrics were added. It helped her to understand why most of the guests needed drugs to get through the evening.

She tried to work out where she'd gone wrong. She'd been forward, true, possibly even giddy, but she couldn't understand why Sally had rejected her as harshly as she had. Usually, people were flattered when she made a pass at them, or at least were willing to indulge her for a few moments. This time, her attempts at seduction had backfired. It was as if Sally had slapped her in the face.

Feeling wretched and seeking solace from somewhere, she picked up her phone. There, fourth from the top, was the message she had sent Robert only a few days previously. The more recent messages were from people who were upstairs, who were now laughing at her, she was sure. If anyone could help her recover her equilibrium, it would be Robert.

Hey, how are you?

She sent him the internationally recognised message which really meant, 'I want to tell you how I am, are you listening to me?' but was more polite. Placing her phone by the sink, she examined herself in the mirror as she waited for him to reply. The harsh glare of the shaving light was unflattering, her face was shiny, and there was not a hint of her make-up left. She washed and rinsed with cold water, hoping to return to sufficient composure to risk opening the bathroom door.

All good babes, and you?

And there was Robert saying, 'yes, I'm listening.' Reliable Robert, there for her when she needed him most. They hadn't spoken in weeks, and she had blanked him only days ago, nonetheless, he was ready to help as needed. Hannah was so pleased to see him respond positively that she didn't pause before replying.

Ah you know, it's tough trying to build a new life

That was an understatement. She hadn't really thought through what she was going to say and, looking at this comment, starkly written across the screen, somehow it didn't convey what she was aiming for.

I mean, I miss you guys

That was better. That made it about Robert, rather than about Emily. Hannah did not want to get into another argument with Robert about Emily. Not tonight at any rate, not while she felt so raw.

Aw, we miss you too babes
What, even Carly?
Well, I bet she does really. I certainly do

Reasonable Robert, such a straightforward man. He'd never lie, but he always tried to show the best of people. As the guitarist and his vocalist kicked into the high notes of a power ballad upstairs, Hannah felt she could do with a little more Robert in her life, and a little less Sally.

Perhaps we could catch up soon?

Hannah hadn't realised she was holding her breath, until she was forced to let it go. Robert didn't reply.

Twice, she picked up the phone to send a further message, but she couldn't decide whether to double down and make a more specific proposition, or to slide backwards and pretend she was bringing the conversation to a polite conclusion.

Indecision led inevitably to inaction. As she stared at the screen she sniggered at herself. Somehow, she had managed to add some rejection icing to her knockback cake.

Have to be first thing in the morning – Hyde's Park at 8am?

She grinned, in relief as much as in anticipation. She hadn't been snubbed, in fact, she'd been offered a perfect proposal.

She didn't want to deceive Emily, but she also didn't want to admit she was meeting Robert. After her disaster with Sally, she didn't think it would be well received. Freddie would provide her with welcome cover, and Emily wouldn't need to know that she'd nipped out to see Robert. Hopefully, an hour with him would be enough to soothe her scratched soul.

Perfect, see you by the lido x
XxX

Hannah felt better. She closed her eyes and breathed deeply, taking a few minutes to cycle her breath

in and out of her body, regenerating herself with every
rise of her chest, spreading calm to her extremities,
slowing the pace of her heart, and pacifying her nerves.
She finally felt ready to open the bathroom door.

And immediately, she tripped over Freddie. He
barked once, leaping up and bouncing around her, gazing
adoringly at her. He had been patiently waiting. Hannah
was flooded with love for her loyal friend.

She curled up on her bed and Freddie coiled in
with her, keeping her warm. As the grunge duo crooned
away, and a gentle waft of cannabis drifted down the
stairs, Hannah dozed off to sleep.

Chapter Fifteen

Hannah jolted awake. There was someone in her room.

Rolling over, she expected to see Sally with a look of disgust on her face, She was relieved to see Emily shoving Sally's stuff into her suitcase.

"Don't worry, Hannah, she has gone. We're sending this to follow, I didn't want her to delay. Not after the way she's behaved tonight."

Hannah was disorientated, as if she were still submerged in sleep. As Emily's meaning sank in, she felt joy flood through her, and her tears threaten to break through again. Sally had gone, and Emily didn't blame her for it.

"Excellent, now you're awake I can pop the light on. I cannot believe you've been sleeping down here, with all that going on upstairs."

"I… I think I had too many Sidecars too quickly. I'll be better after some coffee… And maybe something to eat?"

"Your timing is perfect, Katie insisted on ordering pizza."

Hannah gave a silent prayer of thanks for Katie. In fact, her evening was taking a remarkable turn for the better, and it seemed it hadn't stopped improving yet.

"I'm sorry, I never should have tried to match you with Sally. I made a mistake." Emily's pause was pregnant, but Hannah was too overcome with emotion to notice her opportunity to intervene and disagree. "On paper she is a dream match, but I hadn't seen her for years. How could I have known she'd gained ideas above her station? Quite who she thinks she's capable of attracting is beyond me."

Hannah's head was buzzing, hearing Emily speak like that. She felt as if she'd had another cocktail. She laid back and basked in Emily's words.

"She's heading for a fall, I can tell you. Accusing me of whoring you out? How ridiculous! Of course, I asked what had brought her thousands of miles to my party, if it wasn't too be matched up – she knows the score, don't let her convince you otherwise – and she tried to kiss me. Me! What got into her, the jumped-up little bitch, I do not know, but honestly, why would she think I'd be interested in her?"

Hannah must have gasped out loud, because Emily span to face her. In the light of the lamp, she looked angelic.

"She hasn't upset you, has she?" Emily didn't wait for a response. She sat next to Hannah, and began to cradle her. "Oh my. Freddie's here, on the bed, look at that. You must be very upset to be allowing that to happen."

Emily shooed Freddie away, and he moved to the floor, settling himself but keeping his eyes open, watchfully. Emily replaced him on the bed, holding Hannah and rocking her as she crooned.

"I'm sorry, I was rushing. I'm excited about you and your prospects, and when I heard Sally was visiting, I thought I could make a great match for you. I made a mistake, I see, now, that you are destined for greater things, I need to take my time and let you develop. Look how much you've grown in these few short weeks? Who knows how tremendous you'll be by Christmas? There's no need to rush."

Hannah allowed herself to be soothed. She was in safe hands, and Emily was doing everything she had promised to do. Hannah felt guilty for doubting her new family. Emily's regard for her was high, and Katie was always looking out for her. And if Xe was self-centred and the twins were weird, well, every family has its oddities.

"Not everyone finds their perfect match first time," Emily said, as she stroked Hannah's damp hair. "You know, it truly isn't about the money, or the lifestyle. Obviously, once you reach a certain social threshold, you can relax about that. We must focus on finding someone who's right for you, someone you can build a life with. We'll find you a perfect partner, wait and see."

"I know, I know it'll happen if I'm patient."

"It will, I know it will. I don't do this for me, you know. I don't need to organise my troupe like this, I could be more conventional about it. But I want to throw great parties, and create the ideal environment for my performance art. You aren't interchangeable, or replaceable. You are my art, and I want the best for you."

Hannah recognised Emily's invitation pitch, the speech which had convinced her to join Emily's troupe. Emily had made her an offer she couldn't refuse, but she hadn't considered what benefits the arrangements brought for Emily. Here was the answer, the only currency Emily worked in. Social capital.

"You don't work for me, I'm not sinking low enough to be paying you for your performances. You are part of our troupe, our family, and you'll grow and benefit from us, just as much as we will from you. That's my vision for all my artists."

Suddenly, Hannah saw that Emily was using her troupe to maintain her position at the top of the social tree. Money would make it grubby, it was social connections that mattered. Emily refreshed hers through her art. That is what Hannah – and Xe as well, in fairness to him – were

123

bringing to Emily's party. Youth and talent were currency to be exchanged, given the right marketplace.

"I trust you, Emily, I do. I've no doubt you'll choose someone wonderful for me, and I'll try harder next time to make the match happen, I'm learning all the time."

"No, I mean it. If you think someone will work well for you, you must say. But trust me, don't let your feelings be your guide. It may be exciting to think about soul mates and romance, to believe that love will conquer all, and to hope that blissful happiness is hiding around the next corner. Believe me, don't fall for all that mush. Being led by your feelings will get you hurt, or you will risk settling too easily for fear of getting hurt. Don't play it safe, Hannah, play it smart."

Emily's expression darkened. Hannah had never known her talk about her own love interests, she had always brushed any enquiries aside. Hannah hadn't pushed before, but something in Emily's tone piqued her interest. She was curious about Emily's interest in Farooq, and tried to ask without sounding too obvious.

"Is that what's happening to you? I mean, I watched you at the party, you didn't seem yourself. You were more attentive than usual, I think? Are you making your own match there?" Hannah had not been as subtle as she'd hoped.

Emily stood up, straightening her dress, taking her time in responding. There was a long enough pause for a sense of dread to creep over Hannah, sure she had pushed it too far. But, Emily looked at her and smiled, to Hannah's immense relief.

"I can't hide anything from you, can I? I thought only Katie was in on my little secret, but it appears you are more astute than I gave you credit for. Yes, I might be in a very fortunate position, but it cannot be rushed. It is rather delicate and so, I expect full discretion."

"Of course, I'll say no more. I'm rooting for you, though. It may not seem a conventional match to some, but I think you fit together perfectly."

"Thank you for your approval, Hannah. Now, come, let's get back to the party. Guests won't entertain themselves, will they?"

Alone, Hannah put the red dress back on, and as she fixed her hair she admired herself in the mirror. Now there was no one to impress, she felt more pride in her appearance. She was buoyed by Emily's support, and her insistence that there was a better match for her than Sally.

It showed Hannah how powerful she'd. Maybe it was her statuesque poses, maybe it came from the admiring gazes of those who looked at her, but whatever was feeding her ego at that moment made her feel immense. For the first time, she felt ready to take her place in Emily's world.

The smell of melted cheese had replaced the scent of dope, and was accompanied by happy sounds. Evidently, Hannah was not the only person feeling hungry. But Freddie had not been distracted. He had stayed, patiently, waiting for her.

"Aren't you the best, Freddie, yes you are, yes you are." His tail wagged faster. "Come on, let's go fill ourselves with pizza while we're allowed."

Chapter Sixteen

Hannah was a little worse for wear the following morning. Freddie, however, was full of beans.

If she had known how bad she'd feel, she would have cancelled her date with Robert and stayed in bed. As it was, she'd bounced out of bed and was on her way, before she'd realised how bad her headache was. Thankfully, it had turned out to be a great night in the end and she was sure that, in the years to come, she'd remember the party and not her current, unwell state.

She was still struggling with her injured ankle, and not being able to run was dragging her mood down. Even a brisk walk was jarring, and she was limping lightly by the time she approached the lido. It didn't help that the park was already busy. Joggers and dog walkers mixed with those walking to work or school, a cacophony of people going about their lives. The outdoor swimmers were criss-crossing the lake when she arrived, and Robert was watching them as he waited for her.

He looks good. He wasn't drinking last night, that's for sure.

In his training gear but pre-run and pre-sweaty, he looked like a top athlete who was eager to begin his day's work. As his eyes met Hannah's he smiled, twinkling, welcoming her into a hug. She squeezed him in return, but Robert didn't appear to be in a rush to let her go. Freddie had other ideas though.

"Oh hello, who are you?" Robert aimed his question at the dog, as people do, while ruffling his ears. Freddie acted as if Robert were an old friend, his tail swinging rapidly.

"This is Freddie. Freddie, this is Robert." She wondered why there was no equivalent way for humans to demonstrate their excitement at seeing someone.

"He's a beaut, isn't he? Emily's dog I take it? Bet he needs lots of exercise, he seems full of energy."

"Oh, yes, you can say that again. He never seems to tire out."

"And he keeps you company when you run?"

"Usually, yes." She paused, using Freddie as an excuse to look away from Robert, not wanting her embarrassment about her injury to show. "Not today, though, I turned my ankle a few days ago and it needs more rest."

"You look like you need more rest." He chuckled away. "Don't look so horrified, you still look gorgeous to me, obviously, but I take it you had a heavy night last night?"

"Well, perhaps." She smiled tightly, and politely changed the subject. "Anyway, let's walk on, get away from all these people."

"Sure, babes. You lead the way."

Hannah set a slow pace, trying not to limp as they headed around the lake. Freddie took up his position at her heel, and for a few moments, Hannah felt all was well with the world. Or at least, there was nothing wrong that couldn't be fixed with a little more rest.

"So, babes, not like you to send me sweet nothings. Was everything okay last night?"

"Yeah… I mean, it can be difficult sometimes you know, trying to settle in when you don't know people too well." She wanted to avoid giving details. "But I had this moment where I thought, oh, I miss Robert so much… And Carly of course. But mainly you. I still haven't forgiven her for being such a cow when I left."

"Aw, don't be too hard on her, babes, none of us wanted you to go. You know she reacted like that because she cares about you." He dropped behind for a few paces to allow a group of schoolchildren to pass. By the time he returned to her side, he seemed eager to change the subject.

"Babes, don't you want to know why I had to make it an 8 am start?"

"Because you were keen to meet Freddie at his bounciest, obviously."

"Obviously. Plus, of course, I sensed that you would be dreadfully hungover and dying to come traipsing around the park with me."

"Ha, too true. But it's no problem, really, it means I don't need to come up with a reason to meet you, Freddie's morning walk provides the perfect excuse."

"What?"

Only then did Hannah understand the implications of what she had said. Robert had stopped walking, and although she was dying to keep going, she turned to face him.

"What's going on? You need an excuse to leave the house? Or to meet with me?"

"Neither, I mean... I just meant... I..." She was struggling to find her way back to safer ground. "It's easier, that's all, if I don't need to chat about it at home. There are lots of us living there, and everything is everyone's business. I'm trying to keep a little privacy, that's all."

"Yeah, right, because it's never been like that before, has it? No one was at all interested in your personal business in the home or the squat, were they? Is it me? Is she such a snob she doesn't want you seeing me?"

129

"No, Robert, really, it's not you. Don't start on about Emily, please. I've not seen you in weeks and I don't want to row about it again. Besides, are you trying to tell me that Carly knows where you are?"

"Well, no, she doesn't. But she wouldn't try to stop me seeing you, I just don't want to upset her, that's all." He paused. Hannah hoped he was about to change the subject, but he continued on.

"I'm sorry, Hannah, you know what I think about Emily. She is far too controlling. All this living under her roof, with her managing your act, and choosing your clothes. You're so submissive when it comes to her, when it comes to whatever it is she wants from you." Robert caught his breath and sighed. "Look, I'm not trying to argue with you. I'm worried about you."

Hannah was grateful that he had no idea that Emily was also trying to find her a suitable partner. He would use it as further proof of a problem which she was sure didn't exist, but which she struggled to refute. Besides, as she watched Robert become flushed with concern for her, she couldn't deny she still had a serious crush on him.

"Thank you," she said. "But, please don't be worried about me. And please, don't speak about Emily like that either. Let's be more positive, yeah?"

"Okay, okay. In that case, I'll try again." Robert theatrically coughed. "So, babes, don't you want to know why I had to make it an 8 am start?"

"Yes, yes I do want to know why you made me meet you so bloody early."

"Because – de de de de de de dah – because, I have a flight to catch this afternoon!"

"What, flying off to Benidorm without me?"

For a moment, she was back there, their first and only holiday abroad. Last summer, a late getaway. Their hot skin sweaty with sun cream, drinking afternoon beers together, their bodies too close. Close, but not close enough. Carly had been there too, and there was always the pact to consider.

"I wish."

Hannah heard Robert's wink, she knew him too well.

"No, not Benidorm... New York."

"No, you are not! Wow, how come? I mean, great, wish I was coming too. Wait, Carly isn't going with you, is she?"

"Not this time, unfortunately, but Jane is. She's the new girl at the squat. She's a director, makes films, arty stuff some of it. She fits right in."

Hannah worked hard to keep her jealousy from her voice as she said, "Just the two of you, then?" She hadn't succeeded.

"Not like that, babes, I assure you. Jane's... she's more Carly's type than mine."

There was that audible wink again.

He carried on. "She's been filming me for about a month now, and she's cut this documentary, you know, the squat, the scene in London, the whole shebang, and she's got someone interested in it. Plus, I've been using some of her off-cuts, putting bits of film onto social media, playing about really. But guess who's London's coolest new influencer?"

"No, you're not, surely not? Wow, that's a turnaround isn't it? She must be good." Hannah had not been expecting Robert's life to drastically change while she had been gone. She had always assumed he would be there for her. In fact, in the six weeks since she'd moved out, it was Robert's life which had transformed, even more than hers had. She felt her shoulders slump and her pace slow. She was being left behind as he moved forward without her.

"Hey, it's supposed to be good news, hey, come on." He reached out for her hand, looking concerned.

Feeling him pull her towards him, Hannah moved to close the gap between them and kissed him. Her lips slid over his, similar to Sally's the night before, but combined with Robert's familiar and comforting scent, rather than her ashtray residue. Hannah felt safer with Robert. She was sure that he wouldn't reject her like Sally had. She had forgotten how fond she was of him, and how sexy he looked in shorts.

Robert returned her kiss for a heartbeat or two before he pulled away. He kissed her quickly on the nose before walking on, still holding her hand. Hannah wasn't sure whether she had made a successful pass at him, or was receiving the kindest of refusals, but she was delighted not to be running away in tears. Robert turned to look at her again, sparkling-eyed, and then Hannah knew.

Yes, somehow that was a successful pass. Well done, Hannah. But... what now?

"We've missed you, you know. I've missed you." Robert squeezed her hand before letting it go. "It would be great if you were still around, you'd look beautiful in the film. Jane's got such a good eye. All the scenes examine us through Jane's perspective as she learns about our business. Carly's in the frame as much as I am, but you know how she is about social media. It's really taken off for me, though, and that's why Jane wants me to come and meet these people in New York. They like what they see, babes, can't blame them, can you?"

"Certainly can't." Hannah giggled, glad he was getting the recognition he deserved. He was attractive, he was charismatic, and although he was only a juggler, he was a loveable one. "I mean, it sounds like the start of something very rewarding for you, influencers can earn a fortune from their posts, I've heard."

"It's not about the money, Hannah. It's about the art, you know, creating something appetising and thought-provoking."

"Oh, of course, I wasn't suggesting you sell out. It's just... You can't live in the squat forever, can you? You've got to move onwards and upwards somehow." Hannah was struck by optimism. She was starting to see a way for them to be together, a hook that could convince Emily that Robert was worth a place in her troupe. She let her feelings carry her away.

"Listen, why don't you send me some of the film? I'll show it to Emily. She's never seen you at your best, she's only seen you juggling on the street, you might be able to come join us! Think how fabulous that would be, you and me back together again, and with Emily's connections she could really make you fly as an influencer."

Hannah could already see herself. Decked in the gold dress, looking elegant and stunning, with Robert on her arm, looking splendid in a tuxedo. The centre of everyone's attention.

Maybe we could be the perfect match, after all.

"Woah there, let's not get too carried away, yeah? We're not looking to change anything. The squat, it's real, that's the point. It's a feature of the film, and Jane's got high hopes for it. Besides, what about Carly? I'm not about to forget about her or leave her behind, and I'm definitely not joining Emily's gang. I'm keeping control of my life, thank you very much, and I'm happy with the way it is going."

Hannah was better at hearing winks than warnings.

"Don't think so small, Robert. I mean, sure, Jane might pull this off and you may have to carry on living in the squat for show, but that doesn't mean you shouldn't be making the most of your influencer status. You know, people will pay you to wear things, eat things, be seen places, you could make some serious money with the right sort of following, and that is where I am sure Emily can help."

"I am not going anywhere near that psychopathic bitch," spat Robert, shocking Hannah enough to halt her in her tracks. "Look at what she's done to you. You never used to speak like this, to view the world in this horrible way, as if the only thing that mattered is what you could get from it. You aren't just talking about selling me out, you're talking about whoring me out to the highest bidder. Is that what you're doing now, Hannah? Whoring yourself out in the name of art?"

Hannah slapped him across the face.

She hit him harder than she'd intended, as she'd been stung beyond measure by his choice of words. She whirled around and stormed off, dragging Freddie along on his lead behind her.

She was furious, and she refused to look back. She didn't want to be followed, but she soon had to slow her pace, and limp along. Her ankle throbbed, her hand smarted, and her hangover was worsening, but she refused to cry. Angry, she pulled out her phone. She hadn't finished yet.

This is why I've left you behind. You think small. You are small.

For a moment there, she had forgotten. Forgotten why she had chosen to join Emily, why she had been so determined to leave, despite the rows it had caused. She had forgotten, and so, she had allowed herself to be drawn back in.

Sure, Robert was gorgeous, and kind, but Emily was right. He was not as good as she was. He just wasn't, he came from the wrong side of the tracks. He might gain a little cult status, a few crazy fans, but he was never going to move in the circles she was moving in now. He didn't have the connections, or the ambition. She was never going to be able to convince Emily that he had what it took to be part of their troupe.

The nearer Hannah got to home, the clearer she saw herself. Robert was right, she wasn't the same person she'd been before. She had grown, and she was flourishing. Emily had said as much, only the night before. She had always said she was special, but Hannah hadn't believed her, not fully. It had taken first Sally, and then Robert, for Hannah to see the truth in Emily's words.

Life held promise, and Emily was going to connect Hannah into her social world, and Hannah was not going to let anyone hold her back anymore. She had learned to see herself for who she really was, what only Emily had been able to see before. Hannah had truly become statuesque.

Chapter Seventeen

Hannah held her glass in the air, raising a toast to her new family.

The summer had ended. No sooner had the leaves finished falling, than the Christmas garlands were being strung. The holiday season would prove to be full of danger and romance for Hannah. But for now, she was blissfully unaware of all which would befall her, and she was tipsy again.

"Cheers!" Hannah sipped at her Sidecar, already feeling the effects of the previous three cocktails.

Don't overdo it, you've a big day tomorrow.

The other three were showing no such restraint.

"More, we need some more," bellowed Emily, as she bounced around with her empty glass in the air, attempting to catch a server's eye.

"I've got it." Katie's wave was more discreet, more focused and more effective. "Same again?"

"I'm good for now, thanks," Hannah replied.

"Not me, more for me, more for Xe!" Xe sang and swung his empty glass in time to his ditty.

He wasn't dawdling when it came to these cocktails, but then, Xe was celebrating. November marked his first full year in Emily's troupe. He had insisted on getting dressed up and heading into Soho for cocktails. Surprisingly, Katie had been vocal in her support of the idea, and that carried the motion. All things considered, Hannah would have preferred to stay at home. She was training hard, and cocktails and exercise were not happy bedfellows.

Hannah's confidence in her performance art had increased as her reputation had grown, but this hadn't translated into composure and ease when it came to socialising in Emily's world. Being in this bar was a perfect example of her discomfort.

Hannah hadn't known the bar existed, as it was not visible from the main street. It was that type of place; the people who were welcome to visit knew where to find it. It was poorly lit, with flashing spotlights above the bar, one of those with hundreds of bottles behind the server but no draught pumps in front. The bar was linked to the dancefloor by way of a tunnel, reducing the pleasures to be gained from people-watching. Hannah couldn't understand the attraction.

She also couldn't afford the cocktails they were drinking. In fact, she wasn't sure she would have made it past the doormen, had she not arrived with Xe. He did not share her angst. No matter what the social environment, he acted as though everyone else should be grateful for his presence. He had brought them here for a reason. Here, Xe was the star of the bar.

"I was performing over there when I first saw Emily watching me." Xe had barely finished his first drink before jumping into his origin story, his 'when Xe met Emily' tale.

Blah, blah, blah, blah, blah.

Hannah was far too sober to hear Xe's story for the fourth, possibly even the fifth time. But Emily liked hearing it, so Hannah plastered a smile on her face, and nodded along as if it was her first time.

A few more cocktails and Xe and Emily were drunk and boisterous, and ready to dance.

"Come on, let's work the dancefloor, darlings, show them some shapes!" sang Xe.

Emily smiled indulgently at him. "Come along, then, let's throw our moves on the dancefloor!"

Hannah sat nursing the final vestiges of her drink, as Xe and Emily weaved their way through the tables in the direction of the tunnel. She tried to catch Katie's eye, but she was sweeping the crowd at the bar, looking for someone. Hannah took some deep breaths to settle her nerves, and swore she would make this her last drink. She could hear her bed calling to her.

"Seen anyone you like?" Katie's question snapped Hannah from her trance.

"What? Oh, no, not tonight, though I've not been looking if I'm honest. Are you?"

"Always looking, Hannah, always. Lots of fun to be had, you know, if you're open to it happening. It doesn't always have to be so serious."

"True, I know... But I'm focused on me right now, on my art, and doing my best for Emily."

Katie threw her head back, laughing and taking her time to respond. "It's me you're talking to now, hun. I thought you were trying to "make a good match." You don't think you'd find someone here?"

"What, like randomly choose someone based on how they look?"

"Yes, hun, of course, don't be so naïve, and don't think too much about it. Hook up with someone, check them out, try them on for size. How else are you going to figure out what works for you?"

"I've never really done that. No judgement, of course, but it's not my style."

"Hun, it is definitely mine." She glugged the last of her cocktail and began seeking out the bartender again. "Look, Emily might hook you up with someone, but there's nothing to say she's got a better chance of finding someone who suits you than you have. Relax, have some

139

fun. Aren't you ready for a bit of action?" She nudged Hannah in the ribs, hopefully harder than she'd intended.

For a moment, Hannah couldn't recall her last 'bit of action.' Probably months ago, when she'd kissed Robert. She'd have to go back a lot further for anything more than a kiss.

"Yes, it would be great to have someone… but not a fling, you know, something more than that. I'm looking for someone I can trust, someone who is special."

"Those who wait, masturbate… Look, what about him?" Katie pointed out a man at the bar, dark-skinned and tall. He looked fit. "Come on, I think even *I'm* tempted by him, what a lovely specimen."

It was Hannah's turn to laugh. Katie, though, quietened down, waiting for Hannah to settle before speaking again.

"You know, hun, I mean it when I say, don't take it all so seriously. After all, you train constantly, you rarely leave the house. Where is this mystery man going to come from?"

Hannah twirled the glass in her hand, not meeting Katie's eye.

"You know," said Katie, "if I didn't know better, I'd say you were nursing a broken heart. And if you are, my advice would be, try to get him back, or try to get back out there. But either way, move on. Don't waste the best years of your life like this–"

"That's not fair." Hannah wasn't sure what it was she was keenly denying. Emily said she was taking her time to find the right person for her, and Hannah trusted her judgement. She would not admit to any other motivation for her reticence. Thankfully, she was saved from mounting a defence of herself by Emily's return from the dancefloor.

"Excellent, there you both are, it's time for you to dance! Xe is on the stage in there, it's great fun, you simply must join us."

Katie jumped down from her stool. "I'm in, bloody bar staff are too slow tonight for any proper drinking. Let's see if there's any totty worthy of the name on the dancefloor."

"And you, Hannah, you are coming dancing too, yes?"

"Yes, I mean, well, I think I may call it a night, I'm not feeling too great to be honest." As Hannah could see she wasn't convincing anyone, she expanded her excuses. "It's a big night tomorrow and I need to train early, as well. Actually, I think I should get going."

"If you are sure. Here, take this for a taxi, I insist." Emily thrust a £20 note into Hannah's hand. "Come, Katie, let's go boogie, boogie, boogie!"

Hannah looked at the bank note in her hand, the only money she had. Emily must have mistaken it for a £50 note, this wasn't enough for a taxi at this time of night. But by the time she looked back up, Emily was leading Katie by the hand through the tunnel, leaving her to her own devices.

Hannah exited the tube station and turned towards home. It was only a short walk, and Hannah hoped the fresh air and exercise would sober her up before bed. She couldn't recall when she had last been as drunk as this. She was out of practice.

Hannah mulled Katie's comments. Her words held an implication, a hint of warning about Emily's influence. Katie was mistaken, though. True, if Emily was in control of her love life then she was, arguably, not making a good job of it. But Hannah knew, she was convinced, that it had been her choice to focus on her art and her routines, a choice Emily had indulged.

Hannah's heart hadn't been broken, but Katie may have been closer to the mark than she'd realised at first. Robert hadn't been in touch, and he hadn't apologised. She was still angry with him and had no intention of making the first move to reconcile, not when it was him who had been rude and aggressive, who had been jealous. She followed his social media channels though, his time in New York had looked spectacular. But she wasn't upset, and she wasn't missing him. She was clear about that.

Hannah wandered along the familiar street, its houses in darkness, the occasional straggler making their own way home after last orders. She pulled her black woollen wrap tighter against a sharp wind, and began to dig around in her shiny gold bag. She slowed as she did so, unable to concentrate on walking in a straight line in her heels and seeking her keys at the same time.

Pausing at the bottom of the steps, in front of the door, she could hear Freddie whining. He should have been fast asleep.

"Hi Freddie, it's only me, calm down... let me find my keys. I know they're here somewhere."

She pulled things out of her bag, feeling her anxiety rise as bile at the back of her throat.

I can't be locked out!

Mascara, phone, tissues. "Ah, there, got the keys, Freddie, thank God."

She climbed the stairs, placing each foot carefully, preoccupied with not slipping and injuring herself. Freddie whined again, more urgently this time. She was close to home, and close to bed, and she relaxed.

"I'm home, Freddie, have you missed me?" she said as she inserted the key, re-shouldering her bag before opening the door to greet him.

Hannah was hit from behind with immense force.

She stumbled through the door, falling over the door jamb, and collapsing heavily on the floor. Every ounce of breath in her body was expelled with the power of it.

She felt as if under a great weight. She couldn't breathe in, she couldn't speak, and she couldn't get up. She was coming to the realisation that there was someone lying on top of her.

Freddie barked only a few feet from her head, disorientating her further, but he wasn't biting. He wasn't going to save her. She prayed that someone would come to see what was causing such noise. Whether they'd be in time, she didn't know. She could only hope.

"Stay down, shut up." Hannah heard the words, but she wasn't listening, she was hearing her heart as it raced. She could feel her panic rising, her adrenaline spiking, as pure fear drove though her. But she couldn't move. She had frozen. She was as still as a statue.

Chapter Eighteen

Hannah gasped, trying to catch her breath. She was terrified.

She rolled onto her side, coughing, as her attacker towered over her. He seemed huge, broad, and imposing. Freddie backed away, barking loudly, but clearly as scared as Hannah. The only light came from the kitchen, casting long shadows, and Freddie retreated towards its sanctuary.

There was nothing Hannah could do. She couldn't see his face, which meant she couldn't meet his eyes. Her limited view stopped her gaining a sense of him and his intentions. She tried to speak but was curtailed by another coughing fit.

"Shut up!" he hissed.

She pushed herself away, sliding across the floor, following Freddie towards the kitchen. Passing the stairs, her path was blocked by a large bean bag, and to her horror she rose rather than retreated.

"Shut him up, as well." He pointed at Freddie, who only barked louder at the attention. He turned towards the door, as if to close it.

Her attacker went flying as someone else flung themselves through the door.

The two men fell to the floor in front of Hannah. She knew that her attacker's attacker must be her saviour. He was smaller but he was fierce. His white t-shirt contrasted sharply with the darker clothes of her attacker.

No sooner had her saviour hit the floor than he had recovered, throwing a series of tight punches which brought grunts and howls from his victim. Freddie's barking increased in tempo at the excitement of it all.

In the dim light, Hannah could not see who her saviour was, but she was sure he was winning.

The smaller guy found his feet first, and used this to his advantage, raining kicks into the belly of her attacker, targeting first his face, then his body.

Hannah felt exalted that help had arrived, but was sickened by the sounds of violence, which were somehow more horrifying for happening in the dark.

With a growl, her attacker pushed himself to his feet, hurling her saviour into the banister, hugging him like a boxer preventing a knockout blow. But her saviour was not so easily caught. He used the attacker's momentum to twirl around and throw him through the doorway.

The attacker must have been eager to escape, as he tumbled down the steps and scarpered away. The saviour closed the door, leaving him and Hannah alone together in the dark.

Hannah hoped her saviour was a hero, not a villain.

"Hannah, are you okay?"

"Farooq? Farooq, is that you?"

"Of course, yes, who did you think it was? Never mind, are you okay?"

"Shush, Freddie, it's fine now, we're safe. Yes, I'm okay, I think, thanks to you."

"Oh, it's no problem, really. Hannah, can you tell me where the light switch is? I cannot, for the life of me, find it."

"Sure." Hannah could barely laugh as she was still catching her breath, but she tried. "It's over there, at the bottom of the stairs."

"Strange place for it. Ah, there we go."

As the lights came on, Hannah cuddled into Freddie, hiding her eyes for a few moments while they adjusted. She tried to breathe deeply, wanting to calm herself, but she was still wheezing. Every part of her was primed to flee. Freddie was whining next to her, his eyes unwavering in his concern. Scratching between his ears, Hannah turned her attention to Farooq, thinking she should thank him again.

He was as primed as she, but to fight, not flee. He looked beautiful. His light brown skin shone with a layer of sweat, his face glowing. He was breathing hard, his chest pushing against his tight white t-shirt, which had fresh scuffs of blood across it. His jacket was hanging half off. It looked ripped beyond repair.

"Come on, let's get you up. He's gone, he won't be back. You're safe now." Farooq held out his hand to Hannah, carefully helping her to her feet. As she rose, she was too close. She could feel the heat radiating from him, his breath like a warm breeze across her face. She didn't move, she had no idea what to say, or where to go.

"You're in shock. That's normal, it will pass. Come on, let's get you settled down." With a hand on her back, he guided her to the Moroccan table, wrapping her in a blanket. Freddie curled as close to her as he could.

"I'll make sweet tea, it works well for shock." As Farooq busied himself in the tea-making ritual, he seemed to relax as well.

By the time they were taking their first sips, they were less fraught with the excitement and danger of the fight, and had recovered themselves sufficiently to be able to laugh, and exclaim over the luck of Farooq arriving at the precise moment a man bundled Hannah across the doorway into the house.

"What were you even doing here?" asked Hannah. "I haven't seen you for weeks, and then you turn up when you are most needed."

"I know, right, how lucky? Well, I flew in this evening, I've got nowhere else I need to be for a couple of days, so Emily invited me to chill here. I've missed you guys."

"I'd almost forgotten what it was like, you taking up residence in the corner there, encouraging Xe all the time, prompting him to repeat his talking show, again and again." Hannah acted serious for a moment. "You know, actually, now I come to think about it, I'm not so sure I am happy to see you."

"Ah, Xe, yes, I cannot wait to see him again, and entertain myself, admiring his ignorance as to how others perceive him. It's a good job he's pretty, isn't it?" Farooq's eyes sparkled as he spoke. Hannah, though, noticed the mood had shifted with her pretence, and she sought to recover it.

"Joking aside, can you imagine what would have happened to me if you hadn't been there?"

"No, don't do that, don't imagine, Hannah. You'll drive yourself crazy, and you can only harm yourself by thinking that way. We've no idea what would have happened, and it's best you keep mind focused on not making tonight into something it isn't."

Hannah did not need practice at directing her focus, and she was sure she'd be able to stop her mind wandering. But if she wasn't able to do it, she would make sure that Farooq never knew. It was time she changed the subject.

"How was your trip?"

"Ah you know, family, can't live with them, can't kill them." Farooq giggled. "They were all in good form, thank you for asking."

"Are you actually a prince?"

He took a sip from his tea, taking his time.

"I'm sorry," said Hannah, "I'm being nosy, I shouldn't be asking."

"No, no it's okay. I try not to talk about it most of the time, life there is so different to life here, it is hard for others to understand." He drank some more tea and paused, as if deciding how to proceed, before choosing to close the subject down. "My father has six wives, and many children. He has lots of princes, vying for his favour. I don't want to be drawn into such things. I prefer to be here."

"We are all very fond of you, that's for sure. Emily, especially. She's always saying how much she's missing you."

"Ah, no, Emily will have been happy entertaining herself while I was gone. Truly, she's the only star of her show, but there will always be those who adore her, and I am very happy to be one of those adornments. I know I shall never be her centrepiece."

As Farooq poured more tea, heaping sugar in, she couldn't help but wonder. He spent a lot of time at the house. He was beautiful, smart, earned a fortune in the city, and he had good breeding, even if it wasn't from Emily's preferred old English linage. She thanked him for her tea, smiling, glad he was here, thinking how good a match he would be for Emily, and how pleased she would be when they finally announced their love for each other. Hannah was keen to help this along any way she could.

The sound of closing car doors and merry chatter startled her. "Farooq, would you please tell them, I don't think I can."

"Sure, of course, if that's what you want."

"Yeah, it's better that way," Hannah said, as she headed for the privacy of the shower.

"You poor thing!" Emily exclaimed as soon as Hannah surfaced. "You could have died, we could all have been robbed, how terrible! And the twins slept through everything, apparently."

Emily was sitting low, her arm draped around Farooq's shoulders in a propriety gesture. It was Katie who gave Hannah a hug, whispering, "I'm glad you're okay," into her ear. Everyone's attention returned to Emily as she continued.

"Farooq is certainly the hero, aren't you Farooq? But, oh, you are so strong, Hannah, you don't seem bothered at all. I'd be a shivering wreck if it were me."

"Definitely, me too," added Xe, "although that may have more to do with being rescued by a gorgeous hero, rather than anything the attacker might have done."

"Ah, too true, Xe." Emily chipped in, giggling along. "With Farooq here, who needs to feel afraid?"

"Has anyone called the police?"

Everyone stopped talking and turned to look at Katie, who wasn't giggling. She had asked a serious question, and it wasn't immediately apparent who was going to answer her. Hannah felt they were waiting for her to respond.

"Well, I mean… I haven't called them. I never thought of it… One moment it was happening, the next Farooq had saved me and I was fine. Luckily." Hannah paused, but as no one else spoke, she found herself continuing. "I've never called the police before. It isn't something I ever thought I'd have to do. I suppose, if Farooq hadn't come along I'm sure I would have done, but as it was, afterwards..." She halted, trying to understand herself as she attempted to explain. "Afterwards, it didn't seem necessary, somehow."

"Where I come from you never call the police–"

Xe stopped speaking as Farooq talked over him.

"No, no police, not unless you must, they won't be much help. If you want to track someone down, pay for it to be done, deal with it yourself. How are the police going to help?"

"But someone was waiting for Hannah." Katie was shaking her head, seemingly determined not to let this go. "Someone waited until she opened the door and then jumped her. We don't know what he wanted. It could happen again, it could happen to any one of us."

"I don't think it will," said Emily, "I doubt we'll have any further problems."

"How can you be so sure?" asked Katie at the same time as Xe said, "Really?"

"I am confident that nothing like this will happen again. Farooq has shown that Hannah is not an easy target, and that we are able to protect her. Robert won't come and try to do that again."

Hannah gasped. "What are you talking about? It wasn't Robert! I would know Robert anywhere, and he wouldn't dream of doing such a thing. Besides, the attacker spoke to me, I didn't recognise his voice, he was a stranger. No," she said, vehement, "definitely not Robert."

"Come, Hannah, don't be defensive," replied Emily, "Xe, make more tea for Hannah, help calm her down."

"I don't want more tea."

"Don't be silly, Hannah. You've had a serious shock." Emily paused, checking she had everyone's attention before sighing. "I'm not trying to blame Robert unreasonably, of course not, I know how fond of him you used to be. But, you must start to think about this logically. It all happened very quickly. It was terrifying for you. Plus, it was dark. Can you be sure? Can you remember exactly how tall he was, or how deep his voice sounded?"

"After all, fear does funny things to your senses, to how you remember things." Emily gazed earnestly as if searching for an answer, but as no one else spoke, she continued. "Look, forget that for a moment. Let's try thinking through some alterative scenarios. If someone wanted to rob us, would waiting by the front door all night be the right move? Hoping someone would come home alone? Why bother? Why not just knock on the door and wave a knife at whomever opens it? I'm sure that would be more successful."

"Well," said Farooq, "I suppose he did fight against me rather pathetically. No knife, no back-up plan for being challenged by another man. It's as if he was not expecting Hannah to put up much of a struggle."

"Why would anyone who doesn't know Hannah think that of her?" Emily had settled into her stride now, and Hannah didn't bother trying to disagree with her. "We all know that Robert didn't like you meeting me, he certainly didn't want you to move in here. He has felt rejected and sore about it ever since, I've no doubt. Look, I'm not saying he was going to hurt you, far from it, I'm sure he was only going to try to convince you to go back to him, back to your old life. Although, that would be harming you, really, wouldn't it?"

"Oh yes, Emily. I certainly wouldn't go back willingly. And yes, I'm sure Robert would try to convince me to do so if he could."

Hannah had never told Emily about meeting Robert and wouldn't breathe a word about what he had said to her, but she couldn't deny that this was exactly what he had tried to do. She had been drinking, Freddie had been barking, she'd been disorientated. She had to admit, it wasn't impossible that she wouldn't recognise his voice.

Emily pushed her case home. "Plus, Farooq told us that the attacker was black, and spoke with a local accent. He was the right height and build, and he has a connection with you. Surely that makes it more likely than not?"

"I am not sure," said Farooq. "Although, whoever he was, after that fight, I don't think he'll be back. Of course, Hannah, if you want to call the police, I'll help all I can."

"Calling the police would be my preference," said Katie, her voice softening along with her stance, "but I'll be led by you, Hannah. It's your decision."

Hannah didn't believe for one moment that Robert had attacked her, but she was scared other people would. The police might not accept her word that Robert wouldn't do something like this, not if Emily suggested the scenario to them. She didn't want to cause Robert any trouble, didn't want police calling at the squat looking for him.

"Let's leave it, yeah, put it down to experience. I'll be a bit more careful while I'm coming and going, that's all. It'll be fine, I'll have forgotten it in a few days." Hannah's voice sounded more certain than she felt.

"Hmmm… only if you are sure, hun." Katie did not sound convinced. "We should get a security light, a camera or two, do whatever we can to make this less likely to happen again."

"I can sort that, my company has security experts on the books, it'd be the least I could do."

"Excellent, thanks Farooq." Emily beamed at him. "You are such a generous man, as well as a hero, how can you still be single?"

"Ah, lucky I guess," he giggled, "I mean, if someone as god-like as Xe is still single, what chance do mere mortals like me have?"

"I'm off to bed," said Hannah, interrupting their laughter. "I've a big performance tomorrow, and I really need some sleep. You must excuse me."

To a round of 'night, Hannah' and 'sleep well,' she retreated downstairs to her room. As she curled up in bed, Freddie jumped up and wrapped himself around her. He hadn't left her side since the attack, which filled her heart with love for him. She didn't feel alone, and she drifted off to sleep in mere moments.

Chapter Nineteen

Hannah stood as still as a statue.

She was finally giving the performance she had spent the last month preparing. She was mounted on a low box stage, in the centre of a large room, which seemed to be a library during daytime hours. She was raised about a foot off the floor, placing her at or above the head level of the guests. It was an exposed position, suitable only for a brave performer. Until now, Emily had always kept her one step removed from the guests, by giving her an elevated position or putting her to one side of the room. That is, she was either out of the guests' natural eyeline, or she had the luxury of having her back to a wall. This was the first time she was the centrepiece of a party.

Hannah stood straight, her arms lifted above her head. Her wrists were crossed, her fingers outstretched, her nails painted black. Her wrists were loosely tied with a red ribbon. It stood in contrast to her black bodysuit. Every inch of her was covered with a fine mesh-like fabric, with a slight sheen. This was less flashy, less showy, less gaudy, and less glitzy than the outfits Emily had previously chosen. Hannah liked the look. But, without the flamboyance of the costume, her entire act had to be carried by her stances, and the skill with which she delivered her routine. In simplicity there was truth, but there was also challenge.

Hannah gazed up at her wrists with her head tilted, with her feet placed tightly together and facing forward. She curved backwards slightly, rolling through her spine rather than cranking her neck. She felt zipped up, as if the entire length of her body was squeezed inwards. She gained the strength she needed to remain upright from this pressure she applied into her centre, tightening everything, and breathing slowly and steadily. She had held this position for over forty minutes, by her reckoning. She was going to try and hold it for another twenty minutes.

Hannah imperceptibly shifted her weight forwards, placing more pressure onto the balls of her feet and her toes, and removing weight from her heels to such an extent that she could lift them from the floor with ease, should she choose to do so. But there was no such movement, of course, nothing visible to anyone watching her. One advantage of looking up was that she didn't have to look at the crowd. She was fully within herself, lost inside her own head, and she was happy there.

Hannah began to ease her muscles, starting with her feet. Shifting her weight to the left, she relaxed her right leg. If she didn't stay strong through her hips, she would have tilted as she did this. But Hannah held herself static, straight, and still. A few minutes later, Hannah shifted legs, lowering her weight into her right leg, and easing off on the other side. Her arms were less simple, hence the crossed wrists. She was able to press them together and release, the changing tension in her arm muscles helping to keep blood moving up to her hands. It wasn't enough to stop her suffering from pins and needles. She could improve matters to make it bearable, but she had to concentrate on maintaining her focus, on not moving her arms to release the discomfort. When she had started performing for Emily – when she had held a bar above her head at her very first performance – forty minutes was the longest she could hold her arms up without starting to shake. With her new training regime, she knew she could last for an hour.

Hannah distracted herself by contemplating how else she had changed since then. She was thinner. Not as much as Emily would like, she knew, but still slimmer than she had been before starting Emily's programme. Gymnast training had added some new tricks to her repertoire. Her positions and outfits demonstrated a grace and elegance she hadn't foreseen as possible. She had grown under Emily's skilled guidance. Now, she truly was statuesque.

"Yes, it is, it's her. Emily calls her a living statue, can you believe it? Whoever heard of something as ridiculous as thinking it is entertaining to stand still like that."

It took every ounce of Hannah's concentration not to turn her head in the direction of the loud and familiar voice, near to her right-hand side, and close, far too close. Hannah had not expected to hear Sally's falsely high lilt ever again. Her heart sank with the realisation that, not only was Sally here, but she had come over to make fun of her, to deliberately tease her.

"Would you believe Emily tried to pair me with her? Calls herself a match-making extraordinaire, but look at the state of this one."

Sally laughed loudly, as did her female companion, their voices closer than any others. They were encroaching into Hannah's performance space, and impinging upon her peace of mind.

"I ask you, darling, how could Emily think that I would be interested in anyone in her troupe. It's a band of wannabes and gold-diggers. Of course, this one is young and pretty, but that doesn't mean she's worth a meal ticket for life, now does it?"

Hannah could barely manage her emotions, hearing Sally describe her with such derision. There was no question that she was exploiting the situation. Hannah was the centrepiece, surrounded by guests. Even if she couldn't see them, Sally must have an audience who were also hearing this. It was mortifying.

Hannah's concentration had been shattered. She felt a shake developing in her arms, and all of a sudden, the pins and needles became intolerable. Hannah had to move, and had to move swiftly, else Sally would gain the satisfaction of causing her to wobble. She was not going to give her that gratification.

Hannah prepared to move. She pressed her wrists together, repeatedly, moving a little more blood through her arms. As she did so, she settled her weight evenly across her feet, and began to extend her back bend, her eyes open but her gaze blurred, preventing her taking in any details of the crowd around her, trying to blot everything else out.

In this way, Hannah began to transition. She bent backwards, smoothly, taking her time, not rushing, spending about thirty seconds, bowing all the way down until her hands and head reached the floor. And no sooner had she arrived in the back bend, than she moved her weight onto her arms, centred herself, breathed deeply, and lifted her right foot until it was pointing straight up into the air. Using it as a counterbalance, Hannah raised her left foot, avoiding a wobble as she stretched both legs above her, in a headstand, supported by her arms to either side.

Hannah felt incredibly proud of this switching-stance routine, and was pleased to have it hit the pose perfectly under such pressures. She may not have made her full hour in the first pose, and she accepted that she was not likely to last the ten minutes she was supposed to hold the headstand for, but she had made the transition, despite Sally's intrusion.

"She does have a lovely body, doesn't she?"

Hannah might now be facing the other way, but that didn't stop her hearing Sally, unfortunately. Her companion made agreeing noises, and Sally's voice became even louder.

"Those shapes, she shows herself off well, such an erotic performance. I could imagine bending her all over the place." Sally was giggling now. "Not the sort of girl you'd want for life, but for the night, well, I'm sure she wouldn't disappoint."

Hannah burned. She was eye-level with the knees of the guests, trying to keep her gaze unfocused, concentrating on pulling herself inwards, giving herself strength, but she could not help but be distracted. At the periphery of her vision, two sets of long, shiny legs were closer than anyone else's. They were within her performing space, and would undoubtedly be drawing others forward.

"She looks good enough to eat like that, doesn't she?"

Sally's comments were getting worse. Hannah watched a trousered pair of legs move closer to her. She hoped no one would take it a step further and start touching her.

"But, really, while she might be fun for a night or two, she is hardly what one would look for in a serious partner."

"Sure, Sally," answered her friend, her strong southern American drawl elongating her response. "I mean, what was Emily thinking?"

"Well, I didn't fall for it, so I've no idea. But I tell you, if she is whoring out girls like this one, there must be something in it for her. She always liked to collect pets. They must make some money for her somehow. I know Emily, she doesn't waste her time if there's no benefit for her."

Hannah was horrified. A pet? A whore? That wasn't what Emily was about, Hannah knew that now, she wasn't offering sex for money. It was a fairer exchange. She brought beauty, youth, and talent to a partnership, others brought wealth, power, and privilege. A good match required them all, but didn't specify how they should combine in each partner.

Sally's insults were overwhelming Hannah's concentration. She could sense a wobble developing in her core, and she tried to respond, breathing in deep, softening her gaze, focusing on staying still, remaining upright in the headstand.

"She was a street performer, you know, before Emily bought her. Whoring her way out of the gutter, she is."

Hannah wobbled to the left, over-compensated and tumbled to the right.

"Oh my God!" Hannah heard the crowd gasp. She was lying in someone's arms, which meant she had been caught. She was wrapped tight, and was being carried through the crowds, and she was profoundly grateful to have been rescued. She had been saved from Sally, and freed from the searing embarrassment of having everyone hear, and having everyone see her fall.

Hannah blinked her eyes open, trying to understand where she was, and who she was with. Only when she tried to focus her eyes did she realise she was crying. Her mask had fallen as well. Tears were sweeping down her cheeks, washing away her make-up. She tried to clear her vision, to learn who had saved her from Sally's monstering. To see who had rescued her, and in doing so, had become her hero.

Hannah found herself gazing into the eyes of the silver starer, into eyes framed by bushy eyebrows, into the eyes of Emily's daddy.

160

"Hey, Mona Lisa, don't cry," he said, his Scottish accent twirling on her over-exposed nerves, generating a pleasurable shudder she was unprepared for. "Try to relax, it's over now."

He had carried her from the party and they were now in a much quieter place. She had been lowered onto a couch, one long enough that her feet did not reach the end. The only illumination came through the window, from the busy street outside. She could hear people, traffic, the buzz of central London. It felt reassuringly peaceful.

"Here, don't cry." He passed her a handkerchief, white with the initials SW embroidered in grey on its corners. "Take this, dry your eyes, it is all okay now." He smiled at her as if to calm her, but causing Hannah's heartbeat to quicken instead.

"I'm sorry," she said, jittery, "I can't believe, I mean, I fell... Thank you, I can't begin to thank you for saving me."

He pressed her hand with both of his, reducing her shakiness. "Ah, not a problem, Hannah, you needed to make a quick getaway and I was in the right place to make it happen."

He stroked her hair from her face while keeping one hand on hers, the effect of which was to draw her nearer to him.

"I didn't realise you knew who I was." She had barely dared dream of moments as perfect as this one.

"Well, I know Emily pretty well, as I'm sure you realise by now." He loosened his tie, while continuing to hold Hannah's hand. She hoped he would never let it go. "I may not come to her parties but she visits me often, and she tells me about her grand plans for you all. You might say I have a vested interest in her success."

Hannah's mind flashed back to Katie's comments, insinuating that Emily's father was bankrolling their lifestyle. She should be trying to impress the silver starer, not crying all over him.

"I've let her down badly." Hannah sniffed, dropping her head and drawing the handkerchief back to her nose, "S... W... I'm sorry, I realise I don't even know your name." She looked up at him through her eyelashes.

"Sebastian."

"Sebastian," she said, allowing his name to roll over her tongue, enjoying the feel of it, its resonance. It suited him. "Sebastian." She straightened her spine, lifted her chest and raised her chin, presenting herself to him. Performing.

Performing. Such thoughts reminded her, she was supposed to be the centrepiece for another hour yet. This was her big break, and here she was, broken and humiliated, branded a pet, a whore, and worse, a street performer. Hannah's tears flowed freely again.

"I can't go back out there. I can't perform any more tonight, and I can't see Sally again. In fact, I can't face anyone ever again, not when they've heard all those spiteful things about me, what will Emily say? She relied on me to perform well, she's invested everything, she's helped me so much, to establish myself here, to progress. Oh, she's going to be disappointed with me, maybe even angry with me, how am I going to—"

"Stop," he ordered, placing his finger on her lips. Hannah halted her rambling speech and returned her attention to the silver starer, to Sebastian. She was held in rapture, recalling his stare at her during her first performance. She was captivated by his eyes.

With a shiver, a hint of his dark desires became apparent to her. Again, she saw his wish to possess her and she was captured, unwilling to resist, unable to catch her breath, and with no control over her emotions.

Sebastian cupped her chin. "Now, this will be the last you allow that woman to upset you." He placed his lips to her forehead, and rose before Hannah could answer him.

Left alone, lying on the couch, Hannah placed the handkerchief over her face, closed her eyes, and deepened her breath. With each inhale came a wave of Sebastian's scent, to add to the feel of his name on her tongue, and the lasting impression of his grip on her chin. She sensed a faint hint of tobacco, maybe cigar smoke, underlying the fresh linen smell of the recently laundered material. It was the smell of Sebastian, his scent as he carried her away from the scene of her mauling. She breathed him in.

Hannah was becoming giddy as relief flooded through her.

Sebastian had saved her, he had been there when she needed him. She could not have escaped by herself. She had no way to stop Sally calling her a whore and outing her as a street performer in front of all of those guests. Emily had worked hard to establish Hannah in this society. She was working to find her a match. One with better prospects than Sally had offered. And here was Sally, threatening to ruin it all.

Sebastian was the luckiest thing to have happened to her. He had been stood close to her, she realised now, he was the pair of trousers standing too near. He had been there when she needed him, and he caught her when she fell. He was her hero, and he made Hannah feel enlivened, thrilled, and desired. She was tingling with the after effects of his presence.

For a moment, she wondered whether this could be the match she was supposed to make. Whether the right man was someone who had been nearby all along.

Before tonight, she wouldn't have dared to dream that someone like him might be interested in someone like her. But tonight, he had stayed close, he had been protective of her, and he had saved her. It seemed he was drawn to her in some form.

Maybe, maybe.

"You okay, hun?" Katie poked her head into the room. "It's frantically busy, there's a taxi for you outside, you okay getting yourself home?" Katie spoke briefly to someone passing in the corridor, not giving Hannah her full attention.

"On my own?"

"What? Oh, the driver's agreed to wait until you are safely inside the house. We don't want a repeat of last night, do we?"

Hannah gathered herself together. Last night's excitement was nothing compared to this evening's trauma, but it seemed that not everyone would see it that way. Balling the handkerchief in her fist, Hannah made her escape through a side entrance, avoiding Sally, Emily, and everyone else.

Chapter Twenty

Hannah lay in bed, inhaling deeply, with a combination of mortification and titillation interrupting her attempts to relax and recover.

She was dozing, the handkerchief scrunched in her fist, held to her nose. A trace of mascara decorated her cheek. Freddie huddled beside her, snoozing and snoring softly.

"Hannah! Are you awake, Hannah?" Emily came down the stairs and spoke from the edge of the bed. "I don't want to wake you. Are you sleeping, Hannah? Or are you awake?"

Well, I am awake now you've woken me. "I'm awake, come on in."

Emily proffered a mug, which emitted strong cocoa fumes.

"Thank you, this smells lovely."

"I find there are times when you simply must consume a few calories, and it seems like this is the right time for you."

Hannah hid her surprise behind the mug. There were few occasions which justified calories, at least as far as Emily was willing to admit. If Emily was providing chocolate then she must not be angry with Hannah for not completing her performance.

Emily turned on the lamp next to Hannah's bed, which, from Hannah's perspective, created a shadow effect across Emily's face.

She looks old.

The light was harsh and unflattering, as the bulb was too strong for the lamp. In its glare, Emily looked too

165

thin, her eyes too drawn, her forehead too tight. Hannah wondered if she was older than she let on. It would be a small lie if she was, unimportant really. But as Hannah sipped her cocoa, she realised how little she knew about Emily, and how superficial their conversations were. Her entire life was now cocooned within Emily's. All her friends were Emily's, she lived at Emily's expense and performed at Emily's will. The only thing that seemed to be hers was Freddie. He was more her pet than Emily's.

Emily's pet. That's what Sally had called her. Hannah knew she wasn't a whore, but in that moment, she couldn't be sure she wasn't a pet. Emily had chosen her and taken her in off the streets like a rescue puppy. She had bought her gifts, toys, and baubles, and had shown her off, giving her treats for performing well. Hannah had shown her loyalty in return, defending Emily when others attacked her. In many respects, her life was little different to Freddie's.

But in the process of being trained, Hannah had been transformed. She could see how far Emily had brought her, how much more beautiful and refined she had become. Her performances had evolved, and she had proved herself to be capable of more than she'd dreamed to be possible. She was statuesque, in its every meaning. She had blossomed and become the centrepiece of any party, its main attraction.

In return, Hannah gave Emily her youth and her beauty. Her contribution to Emily's art was significant. Emily had vision but no talent of her own. Even Xe bolstered Emily's life. All her performers lent Emily their skills and she reflected in their glory. But all the time, Emily was getting older. She was losing time to make her own match, and beyond flirting madly with Farooq, it didn't appear to Hannah that she was making any progress on finding any of them their prospects.

Reflecting, Hannah considered it only to be expected that her success would attract jealousy, that she would suffer some evil sniping from someone as bitter as Sally. She could see that now. But her relationship with Emily had also been changed by her success. Hannah was more important now than at any other time in her life, and this gave her the confidence to dream of a match beyond any previous bounds.

"I'm glad you are still awake Hannah, I wanted to talk to you. Freddie, get down… down. I wanted to see how you are, I know it's been tough for you. Freddie, down… I said get down!"

Hannah brushed his ears and softly said, "Go on, Freddie, down," and he rose, shook himself, and hopped off the bed, taking his time. He lay in the corner of the room with his ears pricked, and his eyes on Hannah.

"Anyone would think he was your dog now." Emily perched herself on the bed where Freddie had vacated it.

"Oh, don't be hard on him. He's a great comfort, he knows I'm upset, that's all. It's been really horrid, you know?"

"I know. I know. As I said to everyone tonight after you left, I know it's been traumatic for you. It's only to be expected that you've had a wobble, after all that terror and fear." Emily sniffed her own mug, still yet to take a swallow of it. "I wanted to say that it's okay. There was a lot riding on tonight, and it was the first time you were the centrepiece, so I know you would have finished if there was any way you could have done so. I appreciate how traumatised you must be, it's perfectly understandable."

Hannah let out an audible sigh of relief. She was not managing to mask any of her emotions this evening. She hadn't expected Emily to grasp how hurtful Sally's words had been, or how humiliated Hannah had felt as a result.

"Thank you Emily, that means a lot. Obviously, I wanted to perform well for you, but my concentration was shattered. I couldn't stay still."

"It wasn't your fault. You need to remember that, and remember whose fault it really is. You are the victim here, and it is entirely reasonable that it is going to take you some time to recover from your ordeal. Who could keep their concentration under such stress?"

"I know, oh, it was awful. But I was saved, I keep reminding myself how lucky I was, that it could have been so much worse. My hero turned up when I needed him most, and he rescued me."

Emily was smiling, nodding along as Hannah spoke. This was her moment. If Hannah was going to seek Emily's approval then this was the time to do so. She was not going to push too hard though, she would continue to make clear how much she admired Sebastian, and hope Emily responded favourably.

"He was there when I needed him most, and he was strong enough to help me escape—"

"And how fortunate for you that he was, but also, how unsurprising. He is wonderful, and quick to intervene when needed. Of course, if he wasn't so athletic, he might have valiantly assisted but all in vain." She paused, holding Hannah's eye. "He is everything you want in a hero, isn't he?"

"Oh, he certainly is. Of course, it is all the more embarrassing, having to be saved from someone I was once trying to seduce. Actually, it is sickening, in fact, to think about how I felt back then, how I acted, you know, I mean… I understand now, that I can do so much better, that I deserve someone who is better. And I'm determined to make sure I don't put myself in a position like this again, where someone so unworthy of me is able to attack me like that, and put so much at risk and—"

"Excellent! Oh, Hannah, I cannot tell you how pleased I am to hear you say all this."

Hannah swallowed her cocoa too fast, trying to cough discretely so Emily would continue.

"I admit, Hannah, I was concerned. I wanted you to believe in yourself, and trust that I could elevate you higher in society. You need not sink low, grateful for the first flurry of attention that is bestowed upon you, I have always believed, in my heart, that we would find the perfect match for you."

Hannah was emboldened by Emily's praise, of having her progress recognised. To agree that Sally was now too low a prospect, when only three months before, she had been an excellent proposition. "Of course, I wouldn't be the first damsel to fall for her hero, now, would I?"

Emily finally took a sip of her cocoa, turning her attention to Freddie rather than Hannah, leaving her hanging. Hannah took a larger slurp of hers, to deter herself from waffling on and filling the gap. She was determined she wouldn't answer on Emily's behalf.

Emily paused long enough for Hannah to start feeling panicky, to worry that she had gone a step too far.

What was I thinking?

The tension in the air was cutting through her grace. After all, she had just suggested that Emily's father would be a suitable prospect for her, a potential partner. She took a deep breath, and prepared to row back quickly, to pass it off as a joke if Emily reacted badly.

No, be bold. Push on, make your case.

"I mean… Obviously, I wouldn't do anything without your agreement. No one is more important to me than you are." Hannah squeezed Emily's hand, hoping to regain her full attention. "I know you are close to him, and that it might seem strange, if he and I were to be together. But, if it was something you felt you could support, then maybe it could happen for us. Oh, Emily, you have no idea how happy I would be. He is perfect for me."

Emily finally turned her head, and Hannah was thrilled to see her eyes were sparkling.

"Hannah, Hannah, you are right. You would make a beautiful couple. I don't know why I didn't think of it before. I can see you on his arm, perfectly poised. Statuesque, if you like." Emily took Hannah's mug from her, tutted when she saw it was almost empty, and placed it on the bedside table with her own, almost full, mug. "I do approve, it would be a wonderful match."

Hannah sat bolt upright, energised, like a small child at Christmas. "Fantastic, oh, that is so great!" She pummelled Emily into a hug, squeezing her tight even though it twisted her into an awkward bend.

"Okay, okay, let's not get carried away," said Emily, easing herself away and rising from the bed. "It will take a little time to lay the groundwork. He has saved you, of course, and that will help." She smiled down at Hannah. "At least I hadn't been thinking about matching him with anyone else. To be honest, I liked keeping him all to myself. But I cannot think of anyone it would be better to share him with than you, Hannah. I will do what I can to make this match happen, I promise you."

"Come now though, you must sleep." Emily turned off the light, and leant over to stroke Hannah's hair. "It's been horrid for you, but please, don't feel troubled, don't feel sad. Feel loved, and feel special, because that is exactly what you are."

As Hannah drifted off to sleep, with Emily caressing her hair and Freddie snuffling on the floor next to them, she did feel loved and she did feel special. While she was surprised that Emily had agreed with her, she was also pleased, and therefore, her senses were flooded with optimism. Hannah felt warm, safe, and reassured, which stopped her realising that she had not been as clear as she might have been.

Chapter Twenty-One

Hannah curled up on a beanbag in her pyjamas, eating ice-cream. She was having one of those days.

November had given way to the first week of December. It was cold outside, it was grey, and it was damp. Everything was dull. Even Freddie hadn't wanted to go out this morning. Hannah had virtually dragged him out for their early run in the pre-dawn mist.

Now, they snuggled up together under a furry electric blanket, which had become Hannah's favourite item in the world. Her summery pink satin pyjamas had been replaced by a wintery woollen navy set, which added to her sense of cosiness.

Hannah placed the ice-cream tub on the low Moroccan table, and not for the first time, wondered why Emily didn't have a television somewhere in the house. The house was filled with Tom and Lucy's music, and while that was usually fine with Hannah, today she would have enjoyed the escapism of some mindless television.

It had been three weeks since Emily had agreed to match her with Sebastian, but since then, nothing. Hannah hadn't expected a miracle. She had assumed, however, that she would have seen him again, or at least heard of some plans for them to meet up soon.

She had chased Emily about it once, after a week without seeing any progress. She was desperately seeking some reassurance that she hadn't changed her mind. Emily had simply said he was out of town, and that she couldn't do anything until he returned. It wasn't as encouraging as it could have been, and Hannah hadn't dared to ask again.

And so, she had become despondent. And with despondency came ice-cream, and a desire for mindless television.

Hannah's phone buzzed, drawing her attention away from her self-pity and towards her lap.

Hey

She was surprised to see the message. She hadn't thought she'd see that name on her screen ever again. Not after the row they'd had when they had last spoken. She had thought their friendship was over for good.

You busy?

Hannah put her phone back down, and swirled out another scoop of ice-cream, while she decided on the best response.

It was a vegan chocolate ice-cream, containing a range of ingredients Hannah didn't recognise. It had taken her ages to decide which one to buy. It was her first taste of ice-cream since moving in with Emily, so it was a special treat, and her choice was therefore of paramount importance. She wanted to become a better person, and cutting down on dairy was a good way to do that. A lower carbon footprint, less separating-cows-from-their-babies, and so forth. But then, she was also trying to eat clean, and the greater the number of ingredients, generally speaking, the more over-processed it was. It was a tough decision, and Hannah had vacillated for some time by the freezers in the supermarket. In the end, she had decided that there was nothing clean about any type of ice-cream, full stop, the whole point was that it was dirty. This had settled matters. She had chosen the one with the fewest calories.

I mean now, are you busy now?

Hannah saw no point in delaying her response any further. She couldn't say she was busy without lying, as she was far from busy. She was lounging in her pyjamas at three o'clock on a Tuesday afternoon, listening to classical music and eating ice-cream. There were many words she could use to describe herself, but busy was not one of them.

She knew what her answer was going to be, and what is more, she knew what this exchange would lead to. She wanted to make amends, but she knew where these messages were going. If she answered, she would accept the invite when it came, and that meant she would have to go outside into the cold and damp again. She would need to get dressed. While that didn't appeal to her, she found herself replying.

I'm not busy. What do you have in mind?

Hannah hoped for something indoors, maybe something involving alcohol. She didn't have to wait long to be disappointed.

Winter wonderland entrance at 5

Her heart sank at the sight of it. The Christmas funfair. It'd be freezing. It was still grey out now, but it'd be dark by five. She gave herself a shake. There would be people, bright lights, and music. She could take Freddie along with her, assuming he would allow himself to be dragged out the warm house again. After all this time, and the way things had been left between them when they had last spoken, she didn't feel she could refuse.

Great. See you then

She scooped out another spoon of ice-cream, but she had rather lost her interest in it. She dumped the tub on to the floor for Freddie. She wished she could go to the park in her pyjamas. She didn't want to have to find something different to wear, to think through her outfit, to decide how warm something was, and which shoes would be needed.

Sod it, I will go to the park in my pyjamas.

They would hardly be visible once she was wrapped up in furry boots, winter coat, gloves, scarf, and a woolly hat. She would look good, if rather casual, while wearing her newest winter gear. She wouldn't look like she was making too much effort, and she wouldn't have to bother getting changed.

Perfect.

Freddie was reluctant, but he refused to be left behind once Hannah made it clear she was leaving, with or without him. All wrapped up as she was, it didn't seem as cold and dismal outside. The bright lights of Winter Wonderland were visible as soon as she entered Hyde Park, shining into the sky. She took a direct route, hoping to reach them before the darkened gloom gave over to full blackness.

She arrived a few minutes early, and hung around the entrance, feeling agitated and getting chilly. She was surprised to find she was anxious. She didn't believe she had anything to apologise for, but she wanted them to be friends again. She hoped it wouldn't be too painful.

"Hi. There you are. I was worried I wouldn't recognise you."

Hannah turned to see Carly, hovering a few feet away, looking as apprehensive as Hannah felt. Hannah hadn't seen her for about six months, but would have recognised her anywhere.

Her hair was tied back and shoved underneath a black cap, and she looked chilly in a waist length jacket. It didn't look thick enough for this weather. Hannah had forgotten what it was like to not have the perfect outfit for every occasion, and to look as ill-prepared for an event as Carly appeared to be. While Carly hadn't changed a bit, Hannah had changed a lot.

"Hi Carly, it's been such a long time. Oh, it's so good to see you." Hannah squeezed her and, after a momentary pause, she felt Carly hug her back. Hannah welled up as she realised how much she'd missed her. Carly had been her best friend since they were kids, they were as close as sisters. She held her even tighter.

"I know, it's good to see you too." Carly pulled away, blinking her eyes and pretending they hadn't filled with tears, as if that way no one would notice. Hannah knew she'd be unwilling to admit feeling like this, but she was touched all the same.

"Come on," Carly said, "let's walk and find some hot chocolate, try to keep warm." She strode into the crowds, leaving Hannah and Freddie to follow in her wake if they wished.

"Typical, bloody-minded Carly," muttered Hannah to Freddie. "She cannot admit she's pleased to see me." But she followed, catching up with her next to a hook-a-duck stall which was popular with six-year-old boys, who were clawing at each other as they tried to win a prize. Away from the entrance, the crowd had thinned enough for them to walk side by side.

"Hmmm, well," started Hannah, knowing she would need to be the one who began bridging the gap between them. "Chilly, isn't it?" When no response was forthcoming, she tried again. "Are you keeping well?"

"I'm still mad you left us."

Blunt as ever.

Carly removed her cap and shook her head, thrusting her hands through her hair to pull it away from her face, and sandwiching the cap back on. "So… let's not, let's not revisit it, yeah? I've come to talk to you, I've got news to share. I haven't come for a row."

"Oh, well, obviously, I am pleased you haven't come to row with me. And you did have a reason in mind then?" Hannah should have known there would be something behind Carly's urgency, to push her into

177

getting in touch with her. It had been a long time since they had last spoken. They had argued on a warm summer's day, a far cry from this misty, dark, and cold evening.

"Robert is leaving." Carly stared at her shoes as they walked along, seemingly determined to avoid Hannah's eye. "He has a new job, and he's leaving London."

"What?" She hadn't thought Robert would ever leave London. It was part of his DNA, it was virtually unthinkable. At least this explained why Carly seemed so brittle. It wasn't just that she was feeling cold. "How come? What's he doing?"

"He's got this social media thing going on." Hannah glazed over a little as Carly filled her in on Jane, and the filming, and the trip to New York. It was clear that she didn't know that Hannah had met Robert and, therefore, already knew about this. Hannah smiled to herself. It was lovely to have a secret with Robert, something special, only between the two of them. There had been no such privacy in all the years they had lived together, and it thrilled her that they were finally able to do so now. She wasn't about to spoil that by mentioning anything to Carly.

Thinking about Robert as Carly complained about Jane, Hannah couldn't recall why he'd upset her as much as he had. He was obviously jealous of Emily. That should have pleased her. A year ago, that would have delighted her. She shouldn't have let herself get as niggled about it as she had done.

"And now, since he's been back from New York, all these offers have been flying in. And he's accepted one, he's off to start fresh in a new city, any city, and make a film about how he does that. How he meets people, finds a pitch, learns the scene, that sort of thing."

178

"Well, that sounds promising, doesn't it?" Hannah was starting to understand the problem.

"Yes, I suppose it is good for Robert. But it means he's disappearing, and that leaves me without anyone to work with, without an act, not even anyone to live with, nothing."

Hannah had a heavy feeling in her stomach.

"I thought I'd come and see where you're at, and whether you were ready to come home yet." Carly paused for breath, removing her cap and putting it back on again. "I'm sure Robert would stay in London if the three of us were back together. He was upset when you left. If you came back, it would be okay again."

Hannah wasn't sure how to respond. Carly was usually angry in the face of difficulties, not dejected like this. Hannah's mounting sense of dread became infused with pity for Carly's situation, and she hoped she could say what was necessary without devastating her any further.

"It is a great thought, Carly. It really is. It would be lovely to think that the three of us could be together again. Maybe you are right, maybe if we'd stayed together in the summer this wouldn't be happening now."

Carly smiled at her, and before Hannah could continue, she heard her muttering 'please' under her breath.

I must be firm, it's the only way. "But, maybe it was destined to happen. Maybe it was what we all needed. To be on our own, to make each of us work out what suits us best."

Hannah was trying to say no without having to say no, and it was hard. She needed a distraction.

"Hey, look, let's get some hot chocolate, that's exactly what we need on an evening like this one, something dark, hot, and sweet inside us."

Giggling at her poor attempt at innuendo, but knowing it would be lost on Carly anyway, Hannah bounded over to the nearest stall, where they were handing out steaming mugs of chocolate covered in cream. Ordering two, Hannah turned away, and bent to pet Freddie, giving herself time to think.

She wasn't sure if she was happy for Robert, but she supposed she wanted the best for him. She couldn't help but feel a little piqued that he was moving away and, in effect, was the one leaving her behind. She had to admit, she felt stung. She resented him leaving, that he wasn't going to be in the city, wouldn't be there when she needed him.

She knew she wouldn't try to stop him. She had no intention of leaving Emily, or abandoning her new life. Her desire for Robert was real and long-lived but he could not compete with Sebastian, who was not only a highly promising match, but one which Emily approved of. Robert could not claim her attention when her silver starer was gazing at her from the horizon.

"Don't you trouble yourself, princess. I'll pay for these." Carly had already handed over cash by the time Hannah had risen. She was surprised at how swiftly she had forgotten about Carly. She sensed a hint of sarcasm. It was unlike Carly to be subtle, she was not known for her delicacy. She must still be hoping that Hannah would change her mind.

Hannah was about to intervene and offer to pay when she realised that she didn't have any money on her. She'd become used to Emily paying for everything. Her only source of cash was the household kitty, and it hadn't occurred to her to bring some of it out with her. She had no choice but to allow Carly to pay.

"Thanks Carly, you're a star. I'll get our next round in." Hannah picked off the marshmallows, passing one down to Freddie and casually dropping the others to the floor and standing on them. "Cheers!"

"Cheers." Carly lifted her mug to Hannah's, but she didn't share her good cheer. Her mouth was tight and her body appeared tense.

Maybe she's cold.

"Ooh, this is a bit sweet, isn't it?" Hannah wiped some cream from her upper lip. The hot chocolate tasted like syrup. She couldn't believe how synthetically sweet something could be made to taste. "I mean, it's like it's made of pure sugar. And that cream, look, it's flattening already, just air, sugar and chemicals, that is."

"If you say so." Carly took a deeper draft of hers, wiping her bare hand over her face to clear the cream off. "I think it hits the spot. It's hot and sugary, what else were you expecting?"

"I'm sorry, Carly, you're right, of course." Hannah didn't want to fall out with her unless it was necessary. Not now they were talking for the first time in months, not with Robert about to leave, and certainly not when she didn't know all the details.

"I've become used to Emily's, that's all. She makes it with cocoa nibs, you see, not hot chocolate powder, then there's no added sugar. And she uses milk, frothing it up for the top, and it holds so well that you don't miss the cream."

Carly was staring at her, looking as if she didn't understand.

Hannah continued. "She's got this fabulous machine, it does it all for her, makes it simple. Yeah, I had forgotten how much sugar gets added to things, and how it feels when it sticks to your teeth."

"You used to like it. Before you went and got stuck up yourself." Carly's cheeks had gained some colour. " Listen to you 'oh Emily's got this, I've got that,' you sound like a right dick. Since when do you care about sugar?"

"Who doesn't care about sugar?" Hannah felt less concerned about turning Carly's request down now. They'd drifted further apart than she'd realised.

"I tell you what, you never used to be bloody ungrateful. If you don't want it, fine, I'll drink it, but we aren't letting it go to waste. That cost me a fiver!"

"Well, yes, I know, and look, I didn't say I wasn't going to drink it, did I?" She hoped Carly was too angry to notice the marshmallows.

"You didn't have to say anything, it's written all over your face. You aren't the Hannah I used to know and love, she wouldn't have given two hoots about how much sugar was in her hot chocolate. Being Lady Muck doesn't suit you, stop prancing around as if you're God's gift."

Carly's cheeks had turned bright red. There was a vein pulsing in her forehead. Hannah was mesmerised by it, she couldn't recall noticing this before. Recently, she had been surrounded by less pliable foreheads which she didn't think would move in the same manner. Her thoughts were distracting her, stopping her from realising how angry Carly was.

I can't wait to tell Katie about this.

And with that, Hannah was certain that she had moved on. Katie was her new sister now, the person she gossiped with, the one who would always get her jokes. It was sad, but she had outgrown Carly. She had moved so far up in society that, really, they didn't have anything in common anymore.

Hannah took a deep breath, trying to find some way to make this right to help Carly understand why things had changed between them and why it couldn't go back to being how it was. But Carly didn't wait to hear what she had to say.

"You don't give a shit, do you? You can't even be arsed to put that glassy-eyed stare on your face, yes, that one you think stops everyone knowing what you're thinking. You don't care, do you?"

Hannah felt this was getting a little too personal for her liking, but Carly hadn't finished.

"Let me tell you, when you do that glazed-over thing, you don't look enigmatic, you look dumb. It looks like you're thinking about nothing. But now, you aren't even doing that, you're thinking you cannot be arsed with this, I can see it. You're thinking, 'what can I tell her to calm her down.' You're thinking, 'What's wrong with this stupid cow, that she screams and shouts about bloody hot chocolate.'

Hannah was actually thinking that Carly was spitting at her as she shouted, but this wasn't the time to say so.

"It's you, it's you who has changed, it's you that has got this wrong, it's you who is going to regret this."

As Carly's voice rose, Freddie began barking at her. She was now in floods of tears in the centre of a crowd which was edging away from her, leaving her oddly illuminated as she stood midway between the brightly flashing stalls.

Hannah could smell candyfloss, and frying onions, and she could hear three different Christmas songs, playing at different volumes from different outlets. She felt overwhelmed by it all, it was too much. She wished she was listening to Tom and Lucy play, a glass of champagne in her hand, feeling warm and cosy at home.

"Look. Hannah. Come back. Please. We were good together, the three of us. Without you, it's all fallen apart. You aren't happier with Emily, that's not your world, you don't fit in there. We're your family, you belong with us. Come home."

"No, Carly." Hannah shook her head, wanting to be gentle but knowing she needed to be clear. "I'm not coming back with you. It isn't my world anymore. I have a new home now, and a new family. You're going to have to move on too. I am sorry, I really am."

Carly gawped, her tears flowing, looking thoroughly miserable. "You'll regret this, Hannah. One day soon, this will go wrong for you and when it does, I'm going to be glad about it."

Carly turned and fled. She dipped between groups of people and disappeared from Hannah's sight in seconds. Hannah couldn't have caught her if she'd tried, and she wasn't feeling inclined to try.

She squatted to pet Freddie, feeling rather drained. "Come along Freddie, it's been a long day. Let's get home." His tail wagged briskly in response.

Chapter Twenty-Two

Hannah's hopes of a tranquil evening were dashed as soon as she opened the front door.

She was not prepared for the boisterous party that greeted her when she returned. Emily and Katie, Farooq and Xe, all sitting high and scattered around the island. Sidecars rested in front of them, in various stages of consummation, and the debris from previous rounds of cocktails littered the middle of the island. The makeshift cocktail bar appeared to have gained a few more bottles, merging with glasses and sliced fruit to dominate the far end of the island.

Hannah was feeling strung out. She was cold and her clothes smelt of the funfair; of smoke, candyfloss, and fried food. She could still hear the Christmas music ringing in her ears, which suggested she would have a headache that kept her in bed the following day, if she wasn't careful.

She had jogged home, as fast as she could in her winter boots, hoping to rinse herself of her toxic emotions. Blood pumping around her body should cleanse the bad feelings away, and replace them with endorphins. She was trying to leave behind the hurt she'd felt at hearing Carly's accusations, but to no avail. So, she was feeling fragile as she stepped inside the house, and she hoped for a hot bath, some good cocoa, and an early night, curled up with Freddie.

No one paid heed to Hannah or Freddie as they returned, intensely in discussion as they were, and so Hannah headed straight downstairs. She stripped off her outdoor clothes and stripped off the outside world, washing her face in water as hot as she could bear. She was home, and here she was safe, with her new family.

Hannah gazed lovingly at her bed, but was distracted by the voices upstairs becoming louder. She could hear Emily shouting, and Xe screaming back, but about what, she had no idea. She would have to go to see what was happening, it would be expected of her, but she wouldn't rush.

One argument a day is enough.

She sat for a few moments on her bed. She closed her eyes and deepened her breath, while rotating her head to stretch her neck, moving slowly, first to the left, and then to the right. Dropping it forward, then leaning it back. And then she repeated the stretches, breathing more deeply each time. She felt tense and her nerves were tender-raw. Her bed had never looked more cosy, or more inviting. But the voices upstairs rose another notch, and Hannah could no longer ignore them. Emily cursing, shouting about being betrayed, a glass smashing, everyone suddenly silent. Hannah decided it was time to go and find out what was going on.

Hannah paused at the top of the stairs, Freddie by her feet, in order to survey the scene in front of her. Emily was at the far end of the room, separate from everyone else, almost at the back door. She seemed unhappy. Her face was pinched and flushed, but Hannah did not think she had been crying. Everyone else was quiet and still, looking at Emily, not appearing to notice that Hannah had crept in behind them.

Katie was, as ever, nearest to Emily, hovering at the top end of the island, perfectly positioned to keep everyone served with cocktails. Between her and Emily shimmered the broken glass of a spilt drink, strewn across the floor as if it had shattered with significant force. Farooq and Xe were nearer Hannah, their backs to her, their attention fully absorbed by Emily. They were standing very close together, Hannah noticed, before she diverted her interest back towards Emily. She was at the centre of this drama, and everyone was attentively waiting for her to begin the next act.

"Hannah, excellent, you're home, it's good to see you," exclaimed Emily, her voice croaky and her eyes wide. She was too well bred to have raised her voice, else Hannah would have thought she'd shouted herself hoarse.

Emily waved her over. "Come, join us, we have news to share, big news."

I've had enough news for one day. "Here, let me clean this up first, Freddie will hurt himself if we're not careful." She went to the cupboard under the sink and began looking for the dustpan, conveniently hiding herself from everyone.

"Leave it, Hannah. Leave it! Hannah, I said leave it, Katie will sort it later."

Reluctantly, Hannah rose to face Emily. Everyone's eyes now turned to her. She was the centrepiece and she felt uncomfortable. She changed her mind, she wanted to know this news, and she needed to know it quickly.

"Look, Hannah, I'm sorry to be the one to tell you this… it's not a pleasant task exactly, to be the bearer of such news." Emily paused to take a sip from her cocktail, which had been freshly made and placed in her hand by Katie. "I wish this wasn't true… but you have to know, and there is no easy way to tell you this news."

Hannah breathed deeply and tried to keep her growing anxiety under some form of control.

Emily took a deep breath herself, before sighing. "In fact, forget it, I can't bring myself to tell you."

187

Hannah exhaled loudly, as did the others. Hannah was not sure her nerves were going to withstand being plucked in this manner.

Emily took another swallow of her drink, which was by now half-consumed, before gesturing towards Farooq with her glass. "You can tell her, I cannot bring myself to. It's all your fault, after all, so you do it." Emily span round, unlocked the back door and stepped outside.

Hannah kept her attention firmly upon Emily as she lit a cigarette, taking two attempts to get the matches to catch, before taking a deep drag and blowing the smoke into the air, in what Hannah considered to be an overly aggressive manner. Hannah needed to bring this to an end as soon as she could, for all their sakes.

She looked first to Katie for some answers, but she let her eyes drop to the floor. Katie wasn't going to intervene and help her out.

I should have known she wouldn't, she never deliberately disobeys Emily.

And so, she turned back to Farooq, who was also unwilling to meet her eye.

This is getting ridiculous.

"Okay then, Farooq, it looks like it's going to be you. Are you going to tell me what's going on? What have I missed? What is this bloody news?"

"Sit down, please, Hannah. Would you like a drink?" Farooq spoke too swiftly as he moved along and sat on the stool next to her. "I'd feel better if you had a drink while I told you this."

"I'll make it." Katie jumped to do so before anyone could disagree with her. "Don't let that slow you down Farooq, please."

Hannah could sense a change in the atmosphere, somehow the tension had sharpened further since Emily had stepped outside. It was as if it had all been focused on

Emily, but was now zinging around the room, like the accumulation of energy before and after a lightning strike.

Hannah was in no doubt that the storm was gathering together its strength again, and was about to hit her. She still had no idea what this could possibly be about. She closed her eyes, breathing in and out, slowly in, slowly out, slowly in. The familiarity of the exercise helped soothe her nerves.

"Tell me, Farooq. Nothing can be worse than waiting."

"Okay. Well, see… I'm not sure how best to phrase this. But, well… the thing is–"

"Oh my god, Farooq!" Xe interrupted, loudly gate-crashing Farooq's gentle but unsuccessful articulation. "What he's trying to tell you, Hannah darling, is that he and I are now partners!" And with this, Xe threw his arms around Farooq, squeezing him hard from behind. Farooq looked rather uncomfortable, but Xe could not see this. "And we couldn't be happier!"

"Quite," said Farooq, shrugging to loosen Xe's arms from around him. "Hannah, it's true, Xe and I, well… we're together now. I'd have rather you hadn't found out like this, with all this excitement around it, but at least we were able to tell you ourselves. I'm glad about that."

"Yes, poor Emily walked in on us snogging, oh, she was furious, wasn't she, Farooq?" Xe was giddy with the excitement of it all, and as Hannah studied him, she realised he looked even more beautiful than she'd thought before. Love appeared to suit him well, in appearance at least, if not in character.

"I didn't think Emily was going to stop screaming at us. She called us dirty, would you believe it?" Xe giggled as he finished his drink, sliding towards

189

Katie with his empty glass raised. "Another, my wonderful friend!"

"I don't see what's so funny," snapped Katie. "You've made fools of us all, you dick, who knows what damage you've caused. And for what, to entertain yourselves at our expense?"

"No." Hannah was taken aback by how adamant Farooq sounded. "No, it wasn't like that at all. This wasn't a bit of fun for me, we've not been amusing ourselves."

His head dropped and he pressed his fingers over his eyes. Hannah realised how much older he looked, as if he hadn't slept for a couple of weeks. She felt a sudden surge of affection towards him. This man, who had saved her from an attacker only a few weeks before, and been so gracious about doing so. This man, who had been a frequent visitor to their home for many months, who had been generous with his time and his attention, funny and exciting, exuberant, and merry. Now he looked broken, with Emily and Katie spitting feathers at him.

Hannah saw an opportunity to repay Farooq for his heroism, to save him now as he had saved her before.

"Hey, hey," she said, turning more fully towards him and placing her arm over his shoulders. "I'm sure you had your reasons."

He raised his head, tears visible in his eyes. "You aren't mad at me?"

She shook her head, before realising that everyone was looking at her now.

Katie broke the moment's silence first. "It is okay to be upset, you know, don't feel you have to hide it."

"I don't, really, I don't. I'm not upset. Look, Farooq, the only thing is, I don't understand why you kept it a secret. I don't know why you didn't just tell us."

His head drooped back down again, bringing to Hannah's mind Freddie's reaction to being scolded. It was time to pet him instead.

"But, now I know," she continued, "and I'm starting to make sense of everything. You were always here, after all, it was clear you were interested in someone. I assumed you were interested in Emily, because, well, you seemed so taken with her, and she's the right sort of match for you, after all."

"Emily, huh, as if!" Xe was more than halfway through his next cocktail and was speaking far too loudly. Katie shushed him and looked over her shoulder, but Emily was still smoking furiously outside, ensconced in a world of her own.

Farooq grabbed Hannah's arm. "Oh, Hannah, I cannot tell you how happy I am that you aren't too upset about all this. And I can explain, really, I can. You remember I told you about my father?"

"The Crown Prince? The man with too many wives? Yeah, I remember, of course I do."

"He died two weeks ago."

"Oh, Farooq, I'm so sorry." Hannah could kick herself for being blunt. It was her turn to hang her head. "I didn't realise. Oh, how awful for you."

"Yes, it is sad. He wasn't that old really, not by Western standards. But it was his heart, you see, he was rich and he liked to enjoy himself. When you have many wives, it's too easy to ignore them when they try to tell you to cut down a bit, have a day off, maybe do a little exercise."

Katie placed Sidecars on the island, breaking some of the emotion that was building between them. Farooq slurped his before continuing.

"Anyway, yes, it is sad, but with his passing, I am set free. He isn't here anymore, and so, I no longer need to hide."

"Hide?" Confused, Hannah turned from Farooq to Katie and back again. She ignored Xe, knowing no sense would be coming from his direction. "What on earth were you hiding for?"

"I was hiding the true me, fearful of his wrath." He finished his cocktail in two big glugs and passed the glass back to Katie, nodding for another.

How many of these have they had?

Once his glass was refilled, Farooq went on. "I've always known I'm gay, but I was trying to kid myself that it was just a phase. I thought I'd live in a city like London, travel around the world, play around as much as I like – discreetly, of course – but eventually, I'd return to my own culture."

Hannah felt a little lost and tried to disguise this by sipping her own cocktail. She had never had somewhere to return to, nor a strong sense of self that might override any expectations others might have of her. It was only to be expected that she would struggle to empathise with Farooq.

"If my father had sensed I was even contemplating… no, it doesn't bear thinking about. It was easy at first, but then I met Xe, and…"

As he tailed off, he rubbed his eyes again. This time, Hannah used her drink as a barrier, raising her head back to drink, keeping her chin up while Farooq's dropped, giving her time to gather her thoughts.

Farooq and Xe?

It had never occurred to her. She had been sure that Farooq and Emily were building up to becoming a couple.

They would have made a lovely match. No wonder Emily was upset.

She had been flirting with Farooq for months. He had been virtually living at her house, but all the time, he had his eyes on Xe. More than his eyes, by the sounds of it.

"But you didn't tell us, you didn't tell Emily, did you? You let her find you both, compromised, on her sofa." Katie was practically spitting at Farooq. "You didn't care about anyone else, what it would do to us."

"Hey, don't be such a bitch, girl." Xe snapped his fingers in front of Katie's face and, for a moment, Hannah feared she would break them. Katie looked incandescent.

Hannah stepped back in to help keep the peace. "So, sorry, help me catch up here a little more. Farooq, you hadn't told Emily, have I understood that correctly?" Hannah hoped that Farooq would catch her meaning and talk long enough to let tempers settle a little.

"I went home as soon as I heard my father was ill, but I was too late. Still, I've done what I needed to do there, and now I'm free to start my new life. My real life."

Xe had lost all interest in Katie, he was back to hugging Farooq from behind, a gesture more warmly welcomed this time.

"Now my father is not here to define me, I can be who I want to be, live where I want to live, and be with who I want to be with."

Xe beamed at his words.

"And so, I flew back, I landed this morning, and came straight here. I missed Xe so much, but I wasn't sure he'd still want me, not after… well, let's say he has reason to be cross with me. More reason than anyone else. But he's forgiven me, and I'm elated. Oh, Hannah, please don't judge me too harshly, please say you're happy for us."

Farooq's eyes sparkled. He was in love, and now he could be with the person he loved. As he should be. He may have been insensitive, but Hannah couldn't blame him for his deception.

She smiled and pulled him into another hug, rocking him, and Xe, side-to-side. "I understand, don't worry. I'm not judging you."

Katie audibly exhaled. In fact, the tension had died away, as if the room itself had expelled it with a sign. Hannah could sense that everyone had been reassured by her words, although she wasn't sure why.

"That's very brave of you, Hannah, I'm not sure I'm as accommodating, I must say."

Hannah hadn't seen Emily come back in, she didn't think anyone had, but everyone noticed her now. Apprehension grew as they waited, unease spreading as the moments passed. Freddie whined and lay down by the front door, his paws covering his eyes.

Emily's face was twisted, her emotions raw and visible. Hannah felt awful, suddenly sickened. She hadn't been thinking about Emily, only about Farooq, and how difficult it must have been for him. Only now did she see how hurt Emily was. Not only was Farooq partnered with Xe, but he had pretended to be interested in her in order to be close to him.

Hannah didn't want Emily to feel betrayed by her as well as by them. She realised why Katie was still being stern. It was a show of loyalty as much as one of genuine anger at having been taken for a fool. Hannah could not bring herself to wish she had not forgiven Farooq so quickly, or been so warm towards him, but she eased away from him under Emily's gaze, just the same.

"That is it. I am done!" Xe slammed his glass down on the island. "What about me? I've had to keep quiet all this time, watching you all drape yourself across

194

him, being all, 'oh Farooq, you're my hero,' and all the time, I couldn't say anything. I wanted him, he should have been *my* hero, and I couldn't have him, not for all this time, no, I had to pretend not to care. You think that was easy for me? And now, here I am, making myself a marvellous match, thank you very much, far better than anything any of you have ever found for me, I must say."

Xe was gesturing around himself rather wildly, but he was pointedly directing his angsty monologue towards Emily.

"What about me? What was I supposed to do? Hang about here being celibate, just to avoid upsetting you? Pffft! I don't think so. And when you've all come down from your high asses you'll see what I mean, what I've been going through, and then you'll all feel sorry for overreacting this way, you wait and see, you'll all miss Xe."

"High horses, Xe, high horses." Katie smiled as she said it, catching Hannah's eye and winking. "You come down off your high horse, I've no idea where asses come into it." Hannah marvelled at her courage, cracking a joke at such a time.

Xe was finished. "Come on Farooq, let's leave them to their spiteful misery. We've given them all something to gossip about tonight, haven't we? We wouldn't want to spoil it for them by sticking around."

Xe grabbed Farooq by the hand and pulled him from the stool. Farooq shook him off, righting himself while looking thoroughly miserable. But when Xe took his hand a second time, he allowed himself to be guided to the front door, cringing as Xe flounced a little more.

"We are going out, we are going to start living our lives, and there is nothing you can do to stop us. Shoo, shoo," he said to Freddie, who lay between him and the door.

"Go, just go, I'm bored of you both already," said Emily, turning and picking up the bottle of cognac from the worksurface. "Sidecar, anyone?"

Chapter Twenty-Three

Hannah winced as the door slammed behind Farooq and Xe. Only then did Freddie start barking.

"Shush, my darling, it's okay." She petted Freddie, squatting down to his level so she could look him in the eyes and ruffle his ears. "It's all fine, my pet, don't you worry about it." She wasn't sure if she was reassuring the dog or reassuring herself, but it was having the desired effect. Stroking the dog lowered her heart rate almost as quickly as her breathing exercises, and as she calmed down, so did Freddie.

"I simply cannot believe he took us all for fools like that. I'm so angry with him!" Emily did not sound like she was calming down. She poured herself another generous helping. "Who does Xe think he is, throwing a tantrum like that!"

From her squatted position, Hannah observed Emily. Her hair was wind-swept from the garden, her eyes were glazed and reddened. It was safest to allow her to continue without interruption. Katie seemed to have reached a similar conclusion, and fetched the dustpan to start cleaning up, the twinkling of the glass shards interspersing with Emily's sharp comments. Hannah stifled a yawn, eager to get to bed but knowing it would not be an option for a while yet.

"Right," said Katie, "I'm off to bed, and I'll check the twins haven't gone completely deaf while I'm at it. I'll leave you two to chat, yeah."

Hannah didn't need heavy hints from Katie, she could see that Emily needed to carry on talking, to work her emotions through. It was shaping up to be a long night.

"Of course, Katie, thanks for everything tonight, you've been a great friend, I couldn't ask for anything more from you." Emily drew Katie into a hug as she thanked her, managing to squeeze her tight while keeping hold of her cocktail, waving it over Katie's shoulder. "Sleep tight."

"Night," added Hannah, watching Katie retreat, unsure as to what was coming next.

"Here, pass me your glass." Emily indicated towards Hannah's part-consumed cocktail, her intention clear. Hannah downed what remained of her drink, wincing at the sourness, before handing her glass over.

"I'll make us another round and we can chat, just us, work through what's happened tonight and how we feel about it."

Hannah already knew how she felt about it, but she wasn't about to say this to Emily, not while she appeared to be in such a fragile state.

Hannah took her drink over to the cushioned bench, placing it on the low table, and pulling out the electric blanket from its little nook underneath. Checking it was plugged in, she set the temperature to high. It was a cold night and she felt drained from all the dramas of the evening. She hoped that, after a chat, Emily would be sated and Hannah could doze off without appearing rude or ungrateful. Emily came to join her, pulling one end of the blanket over her own knees, and cupping her cocktail with both hands, as if it was a warm mug of cocoa.

"I cannot believe he's done this," she said, "after all we've done for him. We have welcomed him in, treated him as one of our own." She was shaking her head, and Hannah found herself nodding in agreement, though she wasn't clear as to whom Emily was referring.

"He's only a banker. Normally, I wouldn't have allowed him to step over my threshold. But I thought he was cultured, that he understood what I was trying to achieve here."

Ah, so she's talking about Farooq. Hannah ceased her nodding.

"I cannot believe he has conned us like this. Scammed, that's how I feel. Scammed!"

Hannah didn't interrupt, allowing Emily to take a decent sip of her drink before continuing.

"How could I not have seen it? I'm supposed to be the match-maker extraordinaire, aren't I? And yet, somehow, I missed this going on, right under my nose. Even worse, I had plans in play for Farooq and now look, look at what a mess he's made of everything."

No plans in play for Xe, hey?

Actually, now Hannah stopped to think about it, she had not once heard Emily talk about any romantic prospect for Xe. Not even someone who may be a possibility for him. It occurred to Hannah that, if Xe had not sorted his own match out, he might have stayed performing for Emily until he outlived his usefulness.

Surely I'm not in that situation? Surely Emily has begun to make some arrangements with Sebastian?

Hannah was desperate to ask, but didn't think tonight was the right time to do so, not with Emily being so angry about Farooq. Hannah zoned back into her rant.

"I invited him into my home. I made him feel welcome, fed him, entertained him, found a bed for him when it was too late for him to go home. I introduced him at parties. And I was working him as a prospective match, just like I promised. And look at it now, what a mess!"

Hannah was nodding along again, stroking Freddie's head, half-listening and wondering. Emily seemed more put out than heart-broken. She felt he had

199

taken advantage of her generosity and made a fool of her, rather than feeling distraught about her own lost chance at happiness. After all, Farooq was not only partnered with someone else, he was gay. No matter how things worked out with Xe, Farooq was not going to be in a relationship with Emily, that had become clear. That was the cruellest part of the whole debacle.

Hannah had found herself an inoffensive, middling position to take, one she was comfortable with. Of course, they could hardly be angry with Farooq for being gay. But they could be upset that he hadn't been open with them.

Emily appeared to have reached a similar conclusion.

"Now, I know, obviously, obviously, he is gay. And if he's gay, well, then Xe is the best man for him. They suit each other. You can imagine them walking arm in arm around the park, or dancing in a club together, can't you? So, I'm not surprised they have paired off together. But, of course, if I had known, I'd have been more careful. Oh, Hannah, what a mess this is!"

"I know, I know." She rubbed Emily's shoulders, while Emily held her head in her hands, her cocktail momentarily forgotten. "I feel pretty foolish as well, so you've got every reason to be upset. But I also feel sorry for Farooq, it must have been awful for him, having to hide who he was from everyone."

"I don't know, Hannah, most people hide something from their parents. I don't really see how this is different. I appreciate you wouldn't know about that, not having parents to hide things from, but the rest of us are all at it. We keep quiet about some things, we don't volunteer information about something else. We can always live a bit freer once they depart, that's one of the better things about them dying. Along with the inheritance, of course."

Hannah was too shocked to reply. She had never heard anyone speak so casually about parents dying. Not hers, not their own, nor anyone else's for that matter.

It must be the alcohol talking, Emily is just misspeaking under its influence.

Hannah wanted to reassure her about Farooq but not at the risk of agreeing with Emily about this. So, she stayed quiet, and Emily continued on, as if she hadn't said anything unusual.

"Whatever it was he had going on, however hard it may have been for him, that is no excuse for mistreating you. Whatever else he's done, it is that which is so awful, and it is that which I cannot forgive. How could he do that to you? Lead you on, let us all get our hopes up, only for him to pull it away from us at the last moment."

"Please, there is no reason to be upset on my behalf. Really, I'm more concerned about how he's treated you."

"But, you were so excited about being paired with him, and I had all these plans to do so. He gave me the impression he was looking for a partner, and then you said you were interested in him, that you were in love with him, and I thought, 'excellent!' You were so perfect for each other, and now look, what a mess."

"But Emily, I'm not in love with Farooq. I'm not sure why you think that, but I don't think of him in that way, I promise. If you are only as angry with Farooq as you are because of me then, please, forgive him. Don't hold anything against him for me."

"Stop pretending, Hannah, you can't hide your feelings from me."

"Really, I'm fine. I thought you were lining him up for yourself, as your own match, to be honest. I thought that was why you were so upset."

"What, you thought I was interested in Farooq?"

"Well, yes," said Hannah, "I mean, you were always close by to him, spending time together, I thought, you know, I thought you'd make a good couple."

Emily threw her head back, laughing hard, but Hannah thought she should continue anyway.

"You spend so much time and effort trying to arrange partners for everyone else, isn't it about time you spent a little time on your own love life?"

"My life is fine, Hannah, I'm all sorted, thank you for your interest." Emily spoke in a clipped manner which suggested to Hannah that she had overstepped her mark. "How could you think I was interested in Farooq? I ask you. I mean, he'd be a great match for you, and I suppose in the same way he's a great match for Xe, but not for me. I'm interested in something a little more old-school, if you follow my drift."

Hannah saw clearly, for the first time, that Emily wanted to be with someone like herself, from her own culture, and that even Farooq was too different to be good enough for her. It wasn't Hannah's approach to life or love, but she didn't want to upset Emily any further, so she moved swiftly to placate her.

"Oh, I'm sorry, my mistake, my mistake." Hannah twirled her empty glass, choosing her words. "So, if neither of us are interested in Farooq, then, really, there isn't too much harm done, is there? I mean, he certainly shouldn't have misled us. But really, if anyone has been treated badly here, it's Xe, isn't it?"

"True, true. Here, I'll have a refill as well while you're at it."

Hannah hadn't been intending to make another round of cocktails, and she thought Emily had had more than enough, but she took the hint and carried their glasses over to the makeshift bar. This wasn't the time to annoy Emily any further.

"Poor Xe." Emily wandered over to join her. "How awful, having to sit and watch Farooq be so friendly with me, so flattering and so attentive, and all the time he was denying his feelings for Xe, pretending he wasn't interested in him. Oh, poor Xe, how awful!"

"I agree, poor Xe. I mean, he has every reason to be angry with Farooq, hasn't he? But no one else is hurt, not really. This will be something we all laugh about together before too long." Hannah paused while the blender crushed ice. "I cannot imagine what it would be like to be here without Farooq, and even without Xe, I mean, he does add something to the household, doesn't he?"

"Hmmm." Emily took the drink Hannah had prepared, and swallowed greedily. "But, Hannah, these are lovely sentiments, but I won't believe you weren't interested in Farooq. You told me you wanted to match with him. I was waiting for his return to arrange it. Don't try and pretend now, not to me, there's no need."

"No, Emily, really, I've never been interested in Farooq."

"Yes, yes, your hero, Farooq. Perfectly understandable, after he rescued you from Robert."

"No, no Emily. Not Farooq. My hero is Sebastian. I'm in love with Sebastian. The silver starer."

Emily gaped at her, saying nothing. Hannah squirmed beneath her gaze.

"I thought you knew. I was so taken with him, he saved me at the party when I fell, when Sally was abusing me. He saved me from such embarrassment. There I was, in the middle of all those people, listening to her say those horrible things about me."

She was talking faster now, getting more nervous the longer it took for Emily to make clear what she was thinking.

"He saved me from a worse fate. I told you all this. I explained how I realised Sally was not good enough for me, and you encouraged me to raise my eyes, to think higher and work towards a better match."

Emily was still not saying anything.

"And I thought you were helping me. I mean, that's why I asked if you were okay with it. I thought you were so generous, offering to help me like that."

"I thought you meant Farooq." Emily's voice was low, calm, and quiet.

Hannah knew her well enough to know when she was angry, and she looked like she would lose her temper imminently, if her flames were not quickly doused.

"How could you not mean Farooq? How could you mean Sebastian? How dare you think that you deserve to be with someone like him?"

"Well, I mean… you said I was worthy, that I had progressed so far, and was ready to make a great match." Hannah was panicking now. "Emily, please, I know it's close to home, and it's perfectly reasonable that you feel uncomfortable, matching me with your father. But I promise, I will always try to be the best partner I can be to Sebastian."

Hannah was trying to be as reassuring as she could be, but Emily was still staring daggers at her. Hannah was not sure what else she could say to make things better, but she wanted to try.

"Say something, Emily, please. I know our relationship would have to change, but I won't try to be a stepmother to you, I wouldn't dream of behaving badly towards you, or anything like that. We'd find a way to make it work."

Emily used one arm to sweep every bottle and glass on the work surface onto the floor, smashing everything, everywhere.

"He is not my father."

Chapter Twenty-Four

Hannah stood as still as a statue, looking at the swathe of broken glass and wondering how the evening had turned so bad, so quickly.

"How could you possibly think he was my father?" Emily's voice was low, her jaw was tucked in, and she was bearing down on Hannah. "What gave you that idea? Does he act fatherly towards me? Might you have heard him refer to me as his daughter? Pray, Hannah, do tell me, what was it exactly that put this silly notion into your pretty head?"

Emily was close enough for Hannah to smell the cigarette smoke on her breath. Without thinking, she took a step back herself. She moved one foot behind the other, turning her body slightly to the side, creating a little more distance between them and balancing herself.

Hannah could not have explained what was causing her to feel alarmed, whether it was the tight intensity of Emily's voice, or the strain and rigidity apparent in her body, evident in the way she held herself. It was obvious to Hannah that Emily was not happy with her, but unfortunately, Hannah could not comprehend the lengths she was willing to go to show it.

"I said, what gave you that idea? Don't make me repeat myself again, Hannah. How did you come to see Sebastian as my father, and maybe more importantly, why on earth did you think you were a suitable match for him?"

Emily took a step forward herself, closing the distance between her and Hannah. There was a scrunch of glass beneath her heel as she did so. Hannah glanced down on hearing it, noticing how broken glass and sticky liquid now carpeted the entire kitchen floor.

This is a lot worse than a broken cocktail glass. What's next?

The extent of the destruction caused Hannah's heart to beat quicker. Hannah met Emily's eye. Emily's lips turned upwards at the edges, in an approximation of a smile. Hannah appeared to hold her gaze but softened it, taking the opportunity to look around her, making use of her enhanced peripheral vision. There were broken bottles all around them.

Emily twisted her leg from side to side, creating a screeching noise from the glass beneath her boot. Hannah cringed, and snapped her attention back to Emily. She was wearing chunky black boots, unlaced, as was her way when she went outside to smoke. Hannah was barefoot.

Hannah took another step backwards, feeling her foot come down on broken glass. She kept her weight on her front foot and her attention on Emily, while feeling around behind her for a space to put her foot down without cutting herself.

Freddie was barking next to her. He had been barking for a while but Hannah hadn't noticed, she had zoned him out, focused as she was on Emily. She was desperately trying to think of some answer to give her, to explain herself, to make this better.

"I mean, I just… I heard Katie. Katie, yes, she calls him your daddy. She does, I know you've heard her. It made sense. He's the right age to be your father. Katie said he helped out financially. She called him your daddy. What else was I supposed to think?"

"Daddy?… Daddy!" Emily kept bearing down on her, and she had no choice but to commit her bare foot to the floor and take another step backwards. The spilt spirits smelled sickly sweet and she could taste the alcohol evaporating into the air. It was an intoxicating mix.

Hannah had managed to create some clear space for her first step backwards, but her second came down straight onto a large piece of glass. Hannah shifted her weight forward quickly, but not before she felt the edge sink into the underside of her foot.

She squealed and went to bend down, to take a closer look at what she'd stepped on and the damage it had done.

Emily gripped her forearm and yanked her upright, demanding Hannah's attention was returned to her. She was insistent.

"He is not my father. He is my lover. He is my sugar daddy, you dense bitch." Emily twisted Hannah's arm causing her to gasp. Emily's gold watch adorned her left wrist, hanging below the clenched fist Emily made around Hannah's wrist. It formed a delicately decorated vice.

Emily took another pace forward, bringing her face within inches of Hannah's, while holding her tightly, keeping her close.

"Silly. Ridiculous. Dense. Bitch."

Hannah took a long, slow, deep breath. She refused to acknowledge the pain in her right foot, or the pain in her right arm. She was stronger than Emily, she was in no doubt about that. In a straight fight between them, she would beat her.

But, being barefoot amongst the debris of a demolished cocktail bar placed her at a considerable disadvantage. Besides, Hannah could not believe that there wasn't something she could say, some explanation she could provide, some way of making this less awful.

So, Hannah breathed deeply, turned her focus away from the barking dog and her bleeding foot, and concentrated everything she had towards conciliation.

"I'm so sorry, I had no idea," said Hannah, "I would never, it wouldn't even enter my head. I never, no, of course if I'd known you were interested in him–"

"With him, Hannah, I'm with him." Emily squeezed Hannah's arm tighter, twisting it a little more. "This isn't one of your silly pairing games, all bright and ditzy about what the future may hold. *You* might need some man to make you feel you are worthwhile, to rescue you from your shitty little life, but I don't. I'm not interested in him, I'm with him. He is my partner, we're simply discreet."

"I had it all wrong. I didn't know. I know now. I'll keep clear away. I'll never mention it again."

"You naïve little bitch. You don't get to throw yourself at my partner, and then pass it off as a mix-up. What on earth possessed you?"

Don't answer that, don't answer that.

Hannah circled her wrist gently, hoping Emily's pressure would drop off as she continued her rant.

"How did you get such an exaggerated sense of your own self-worth? How did you find yourself believing you could be with a man like Sebastian? That he would even look at you in that way, under any circumstances?"

Hannah breathed in, and breathed out, trying to maintain control of her emotions. Slowly, she breathed in, and breathed out. Emily was still staring at her, still too close, still gripping her too tightly.

"Why would he be interested in a whore I found on the streets?"

Emily paused. Hannah waited. Freddie barked. The front door opened.

Hannah twirled her head around in time to see the back of Tom and Lucy as they left, letting the door slam behind them.

It was clear to Hannah that no one would intervene to help her. She was on her own.

"They know how to keep a low profile, those two," said Emily. "You could learn a lot from them. They know their worth, and they know their limitations. What happened to you, Hannah? How do you not know yours?"

Freddie's barking was now rhythmic, metronomically timing the beats between Emily's insults, which were cutting Hannah as painfully as the glass beneath her foot.

"Have I not taught you to know your place? Just because I don't think you should be with that darkie Robert doesn't mean I think you're a high society chick who can take her pick of the cream of the London scene. When it comes to it, you're still the hired help, after all."

Hannah couldn't breathe. She couldn't breathe in, and she couldn't breathe out. Pain was pulsing through her foot and her hand had gone numb. Her mask was shattered, her emotions were laid bare. She had been shredded to pieces by Emily's racist and demeaning descriptions of Robert.

Robert. A man who had only ever cared for her. Who had always been there for her when she needed him. A person who would never behave towards her in the way Emily was doing now. A man who was beautiful, in every way. A man she suddenly missed.

Hannah could now see clearly. She saw that Emily was not beautiful. She saw that she was not refined. She was not generous. She wasn't the belle of the ball. She wasn't pleasant and accommodating.

She didn't have Hannah's best interests at heart. She was catty. She was calculating. She was controlling.

She had castigated her for her background. She forced her to distance herself from her childhood friends.

She had convinced Hannah that she deserved a better life than the one she had. She'd dangled this future life in front of her to keep her pliant. She'd kept Hannah begging like a well-trained dog, hoping for a few scraps from Emily's table.

Hannah thumped Emily square in the face.

She punched Emily hard, hoping to break her nose. She had to use her left fist to hit her, and the angle wasn't perfect, but Hannah was sure she'd struck true.

In response, Emily's vice flew open, releasing Hannah as she pulled her hands back in front of her face and retreated, shrieking.

"What makes you think you can behave like that? I *own* you."

Hannah was finally able to squat down, and place her right foot on top of her left thigh. She could get a better look at the damage while keeping her eye on Emily. It was a position worthy of one of Hannah's routines.

Tentatively, she pulled a shard of glass from the archway of her foot, rubbing it to check for other slivers before standing up straight again. Her blood dripped to the floor, its piercing iron tang mixing with the alcoholic fumes of the spilt cognac.

Hannah swayed, stunned. Emily started again.

"What, you don't agree? You think you're special enough that all this is gifted to you, for no reason, no expectations in return?"

Emily retreated, drawing back towards the rear of the kitchen. She was bleeding from her nose. Hannah felt deeply satisfied to see this. She hoped the plastic surgery that Emily would need would be ridiculously painful as well as ridiculously expensive.

" Do you think you can turn on me now, that you can pretend you're above all this somehow? You are mine, and I'll pair you with whomever I choose. And you'll be grateful because, after all, what else do you have?"

Emily was smiling, which unnerved Hannah. So, she didn't laugh about Emily's nose, or try to disagree with her. She waited, quiet, wary of Emily's anger and what she would do next. Hannah tried to slow her palpitating heart by breathing slowly in and breathing slowly out.

"Let me show you what I mean, let's make this a teachable moment, shall we?"

Emily darted forward and Hannah jumped back, but it was Freddie whom Emily was after. She grabbed him and dragged him back by his collar.

Freddie yelped as he was yanked over the broken glass. His squeals were unbearable. Hannah's heart skipped two beats before sinking, twisting her stomach and bringing bile into her throat. Emily was hurting Freddie, because of her.

"This dog. This fucking dog. Whose dog is this, Hannah? Is it your dog? Is it fuck. This is my dog. You have spoiled him. You have enticed him. You've allowed him onto your bed. You've lured him away from me. You've stolen him, and you think of him as your dog now, don't you?"

"No, Emily, please," beseeched Hannah. "Please, no, you're hurting Freddie, please let him go. His paws, the glass, look at him. Please don't hurt him. Please!"

"Excellent, Hannah, you are starting to see my point. You have stolen my dog, and you have tried to steal Sebastian from me."

Hannah shook her head violently, tears rolling down her face as she pleaded with Emily.

"No, Hannah, don't deny it, don't insult me any further. I don't care what you say you knew about, what you say you didn't know about... Sebastian is mine, and Freddie is mine. You have to know that you can't have them."

Emily bent down to Freddie's level, bringing her face close to his. She kept her grip on his collar.

Freddie's eyes were downcast, his ears laid back. He was trying to back away and move his head down, but Emily wouldn't let him break free.

Emily pulled him closer to her, while picking up the broken bottom of a bottle of gin. She held the heel of the bottle in her hand, with three sharp spikes of glass sticking upwards.

"No," screamed Hannah, finally seeing the danger and trying to intervene.

Too late. Her arms were gripped from behind. She was hauled backwards, towards the stairs, away from Freddie, who looked smaller and smaller, and who was whining louder and louder.

He started twisting, trying to turn out of Emily's grasp. He was growling but not biting. Either he could not sense the danger he was in, or he was too controlled by his training to react as he should.

Hannah stumbled backwards and fell, landing heavily on top of Katie. She freed one of her arms as they tumbled, but she knew already she was too late. She was as vulnerable and naïve as Freddie, and as powerless.

Emily shoved the broken glass bottle into Freddie's neck, spitefully rotating it as she did so.

He squealed and heaved himself away, knocking Emily off her feet. She lay there, laughing.

Freddie bolted the remaining few feet to the back door, away from the people, with the broken bottle stuck in his dark fur. He turned to face them, silent now, blood pouring from his neck, as close to the door as he could be, before first sitting, and then lying on the floor.

He laid his head on his paws, angled so that the glass bottle pointed to the sky, his eyes fixed on Hannah's. His tail faintly wagged, and then he closed his eyes.

Hannah screamed and screamed.

Chapter Twenty-Five

Hannah lay on the cold tiled floor, her head buried in Freddie's fur.

Hannah was hot and sticky, but she did not want to let Freddie go. Her body shook with her gasps, the tears continuing to come.

She had lain down with Freddie while his blood pumped from his wounds. It had slowed to a pulsing flow, before slackening off. Hannah didn't think there was any blood left in Freddie's body. It formed a large puddle around them both, mixing at its edges with the spilt spirits.

Finally able to catch her breath as her anguished howls subsided, her mind raced.

How has it come to this? This can't be real. Freddie. My darling Freddie.

Freddie hadn't hurt anyone. He couldn't hurt anyone. He couldn't even hurt Emily as she scared him, injured him, killed him.

Racked by a further round of cries, Hannah pictured, once again, Emily pushing the bottle into Freddie's throat. The light glinting from the jagged edges. Freddie's frantic attempts to twist free. His high-pitched shriek as the glass pierced his skin. This time, though, Hannah also saw the smile on Emily's face.

Emily had been grinning as she struck Freddie, and then she laughed. She had been triumphant, as if relishing her power over them all. She was reminding them of their place.

Hannah's body was shaking, she felt colder, as this moment of revelation washed over her.

She wasn't surprised.

Sickened, horrified, revolted, heart-broken, but not surprised.

How long have I been kidding myself?

Hannah loved her new life. She had allowed herself to be distracted by the wealth, the compliments, and the pleasures of life with Emily. She had confused this sense of ease with believing that Emily had her best interests at heart. She had been completely taken in by her.

Hannah had dismissed every warning sign, rejected her friends' concerns, and silenced any niggles of doubt she'd had. As she lay there, wrapped in Freddie's remains, she realised she had thought herself strong enough to cope if something turned out to be amiss.

She had been wrong.

She had also been betrayed.

Emily had laughed as Freddie died, but she hadn't been looking at Hannah while she screamed her distress. She had been watching Katie. She'd been colluding with Katie.

Katie was as complicit as Emily. She had held her back. Hannah could have saved Freddie. She knew she could have intervened in time, had Katie not gripped her by the arms.

Katie had known what was happening, and was as much to blame as Emily.

Katie had taken Hannah by surprise.

Hannah's skin prickled, feeling her fear return. Emily, she could understand. She had made her point and she wouldn't return until it had all been tidied away. Katie would come to clean up after Emily.

Hannah lifted her head from Freddie's sticky fur coat. There was no one there. Through eyes made bleary by tears, she surveyed the medley of mess. Broken glass

– some green, some clear – cut fruit, straws, stems from glasses, the strainer they used when they made cocktails. Beyond the kitchen, there seemed to be no signs of a disturbance. Hannah couldn't believe that her life had been destroyed, but the ripples hadn't travelled more than a few feet from her. It showed how insignificant she was. Hannah lay her head back down on the floor, and tried to establish how she felt.

A gaping hole represented the place in her heart which Freddie had occupied. She felt torn open by the loss of her companion. Freddie had been at her side for many months, and the thought of being without him was too horrid to contemplate. But, around the edges of her grief, Hannah could discern other emotions, feelings she probed as she lay there, covered in Freddie's blood.

Hannah felt shame. Shame at her childish behaviour about her silver starer. Her hero. The thought of her infatuation mortified her now. How could she have taken herself so seriously? How could she have allowed a fantasy to grow out of control until she had made it seem real?

Hannah's humiliation blossomed as she pictured each of her performances for Emily in turn. Each risqué outfit, each suggestive posture. Wealth had painted a gloss over it, but from Hannah's current position, it seemed unforgivably grubby and crass.

It's only whoring if you need the money.

The joke was on her. Hannah was a pet, like Freddie. As Sally had said. Owned by Emily, to be treated well or poorly, at her whim, however it suited her in that moment.

Worse. Hannah was surrounded by people who would not help her.

Her resolve began to grow. Whatever else happened, she was not going to stay in the house, was not

219

going to remain with Emily, pretending that the row had been forgotten, had been swept away with the rest of the debris. She didn't know how she would escape, or where she was going to go, but she was leaving as soon as she could. It was time for Hannah to renew herself.

Hannah sat up and placed Freddie's head in her lap, stroking his nose as she did so, scrunching his ears in her hands for one last time. She rolled his eyelids closed, unwilling to see his death stare. She took hold of the glass and tried to remove it from Freddie's neck. It was an abomination, stuck there in his throat. But it was slippery with blood, and she couldn't get sufficient purchase to tease it out. So, she shuffled away and let Freddie's head rest on the floor. He was starting to stiffen, which surprised Hannah. Briefly, she wondered how long she had lain there.

Her head snapped around as she heard a tinkling of glass. There, stood Katie.

"Hey, hun, how are you doing?" Katie's tone reminded Hannah of someone speaking to a small child.

Is that how she sees me? Has she always spoken to me like that?

"Are you ready to get up yet? You've been there for a while." Katie retreated behind the island, bending by the sink. She returned carrying the dustpan and brush, on its second outing of the evening. "There's no rush, you know, hun, you can stay there as long as you like, as long as you need. I'll start cleaning up at this end."

Hannah stared at her. She seemed so normal, so unperturbed. A rush of anger pumped through Hannah. Her desire for revenge was strong, but she wouldn't be fighting any more. She had one mission, and that was to leave. And she had one fear which held her fury in check.

The last twenty-four hours had shaken Hannah's confidence in her judgement. She couldn't be sure she understood the stakes, that she could spot the dangers she faced. So, she wasn't sure it would be easy to leave.

Katie began sweeping. She brushed glass and sticky liquid into the pan, then emptied it into a bag she had placed in a bucket. She worked methodically, starting from the far end. It would take time before she was close to Hannah, close to Freddie. Hannah was under no illusions. She was going to clean it all away. By the time the sun came up, there would be no evidence left. No one else would see what had happened to Freddie. They wouldn't be told, and if she tried to say something, they wouldn't listen. Everyone was owned by Emily.

"Don't judge Emily too harshly, hun. She has her moments, we both know that, it's part of her artistic temperament. All we can do is limit the damage when it happens."

"She killed Freddie," Hannah's voice cracked, but she didn't care. She hadn't expected Katie to be openly sympathetic towards Emily, not after such an abysmal act.

"I know it's sad, that it's painful now, but this will pass."

"You helped her, you're helping her now. Aren't you ashamed of yourself?"

"Not really, hun." Katie huffed and fiddled with her hair. "Look, Hannah, don't over-think things. This is Emily's family, and we all have our role to play. I've always said you can say no if you aren't comfortable. Have you ever said no to Emily?"

Hannah wanted to prove Katie wrong, but her memory wouldn't provide her with any examples.

I'm sure there are plenty. Why can't I think of any?

"I'm the fixer, Hannah, that's my role in this family. And it's moments like this when I'm tested. I'm not pretending it's easy." Katie paused as Hannah snorted. "Don't start thinking you can make it on your own. You're too young to understand how the world works, so trust me when I say, it really does matter who you know, and how well disposed they are towards you."

Hannah didn't trust herself to reply. Katie dropped her head to the side and softened her tone.

"You might think this has ruined everything, but it hasn't, I promise you that. Emily will regain her good opinion of you soon."

Hannah wasn't reassured. "And Freddie? How is Freddie going to regain Emily's good opinion, eh?"

"As I said, it's very sad about Freddie. But I'm sure Emily will get another dog before long. She's a big fan of dogs, you know."

Hannah picked her way through the glass to move around the island, taking the other route to the sink, keen to avoid having to pass close to Katie. Hannah washed her hands. The blood rinsed down the plughole, swirling around as it gurgled away. Her hands were coming clean, but there was a reddish-brown stain around her fingernails. It looked like body paint, as if Hannah were to perform at some macabre party. She was drenched in Freddie's blood. Her pyjamas were ruined.

"Just strip them off and leave them there, Hannah. I'll burn them later with everything else." Katie meant Freddie. She would cremate him. Hannah swallowed bile quickly, disgusted at the thought that Freddie could be cleaned away and then replaced. She needed to get away from this house, to escape as quickly as she could.

Hannah felt tears building up again. She blinked desperately, trying to regain her composure, wanting to mask her emotions before she trusted herself to speak. She nodded, presuming that Katie would see her. Hannah needed Katie to believe she was compliant, and would do as she was told.

Hannah was about to flee from another family. Her survival instincts had been well honed through her many attempts to fit into a family, only to suffer their eventual rejection of her. She had been lured into thinking that this time was different, but it had turned out to be the same. And so, Hannah would do what she had always done. Mask her emotions, watch and wait, make her move when she could. Above all, keep herself safe.

She needed to change the dynamic in the room, to lower Katie's hackles but not so much as to alert her. So, she pulled her pyjama top over her head, dumping it on the floor next to her.

Katie looked up at her movement, saw Hannah's part-naked form, and let her eyes drift to her breasts.

Hannah loosened her pyjama bottoms, shimmying her body side-to-side to drop them to the floor to meet her top.

Hannah didn't feel exposed as she stood naked in the kitchen. It felt freeing. A first step towards regaining her sense of self and fleeing.

As much as it empowered her, it also relaxed Katie, who interpreted her nakedness as a sign of trust, of closeness, with a hint of eagerness to please.

Hannah halted before leaving the kitchen, unable to resist looking back once more. She saw the true horror of Freddie's death as she took in the scene from her new vantage point. There was blood on the ceiling. There was blood on the wall. There was a flood of blood on the floor, with Freddie's body lying still and stiff in the middle. He had exsanguinated.

"God, what a mess," Hannah said, allowing her emotion to strain her voice a little. "I mean, it's going to take a lot of cleaning up, isn't it? I'm sorry I can't help you… I cannot bring myself to do it, I'm afraid." Hannah placed her hands over her face and sobbed loudly, shaking her whole, naked body as she did so.

"Oh, Hannah, no, of course not, hun. Look, let me sort all this out, you get yourself to bed."

"Are you sure?"

"Of course. I'll be here all night, I've no doubt, so you must say if you need anything." Katie bent to empty the pan, pausing at the sound of smashing glass, as the debris in the pan collided with that in the bucket. Katie rose up and looked at Hannah, who was stood as still as a statue. "In the morning, you can talk to Emily, and you'll see. Things will right themselves quicker than you think."

"Thanks, Katie. Night."

Hannah walked downstairs and stared at her reflection in the mirror. Naked, blood-streaked, but determined. She saw herself as taller, stronger, indomitable, and resolute. She was statuesque. And she was about to flee.

Chapter Twenty-Six

Hannah checked one last time that she looked the part. Ready to run, but not to run away.

Hannah had devised her plan in the shower, while being pounded by hot water. She stayed there for most of the night, grateful for Emily's never-ending hot water supply. She washed her hair four times. There hadn't been any bloody water circling the drain after the third wash, but Hannah wasn't taking any chances. She scrubbed repeatedly, removing every trace of Freddie's blood from her body. She wanted every reminder of the trauma to be gone.

By the time she emerged, she knew there would be nothing left of him. No blood, no body. Only memories. She was determined that she would never forget him, he had been her truest companion. There would be time to mourn him when she was safe, but to make her escape, she needed to stay focused.

She couldn't sneak away. Her window was barred. Many basement windows in this street were, so she'd never given it any thought before. They stopped burglars creeping in, but they also stopped her crawling out. If she was going, it would need to be through the front door.

Earlier, Hannah had tiptoed up the first few steps, enough to hear Katie clattering about while a radio played classical music at a low volume. Katie was true to her word, she was cleaning all night long. It wouldn't be possible to sneak out when Katie wasn't paying attention.

Hannah could not control herself. She wouldn't be able to mask her emotions if she came face to face with

Emily. It had been challenging enough with Katie. Usually, she could keep a straight face no matter how horrid the insult, but this had broken her resolve. Freddie's memory deserved more from her. She needed to leave. She couldn't bear to be there a moment longer than necessary.

So, Hannah was going to try for the only other option. She would be open about leaving the house, but appear to be doing so temporarily. She wasn't certain that it would work. It was possible that Katie would prevent her from leaving the house at all.

Hannah had rehearsed likely scenarios while in the shower. They ranged from Katie insisting she speak with Emily first, through to planning to sacrifice her at a sadistic ceremony. Hannah was willing to admit she was not at her most rational at the moment. Hatred and grief coursed through her. She felt a physical urge to fight rather than flee, which she had to wrestle under control.

Most likely, Katie would accept Hannah's behaviour because it was as she expected it to be. Katie had asked her to gain some perspective, and said that Emily would get another dog soon. While this seemed horrific to Hannah, Katie seemed to believe this was reasonable. Hannah hoped that carrying on as normal would be what Katie expected and that meant that she wouldn't be suspicious.

Hannah prepared her running pack with particular care. She always took her keys and phone. Sadly, she had no need for dog treats or poo bags anymore. She thought her heart would burst as she removed them. She hadn't fully accepted that Freddie wouldn't be running alongside her ever again. Instead, she hoped his spirit would flee with her.

She hid her keys inside the pocket of a jacket which she stuffed at the bottom of the wardrobe, behind a dozen bags and some shoes. They wouldn't be found for some time, but when they were it would become obvious that she had deliberately fled. Experience had taught her that the police don't look so hard for missing people when they know you left willingly, so it helped to leave a clue behind. By the time she was missed, and certainly by the time they realised she had left for good, Hannah expected to be far away from Emily and her performance troupe.

Hannah placed £450 in fifty-pound notes in her pack and covered them with her phone and a single poo bag. She hadn't grabbed every available note from the household kitty, but she had made sure she had sufficient for her immediate needs. A slight of hand was all that was needed, sliding the cutlery draw open as Katie emptied her dustpan into the bucket. She had palmed the cash, naked as she was, and had been able to squirrel it downstairs with her. She was nervous that the cash would be missed before she could leave. Anyone could help themselves to it, but if Katie noticed, it would be harder to slip out undetected. She had no option but to try.

Finally, Hannah secreted her most treasured possession – her passport. It was the one thing she absolutely must take with her, and it was worth taking some risks for. She had renewed herself many times, and she could do anything and go anywhere if she had her passport, a little cash, and some resolve.

It wouldn't fit in the running pack, and it couldn't be glimpsed by Katie, so Hannah became creative. She put on a bra and a cropped top, placing her passport under them, between her shoulder-blades. It fitted well there, quite snugly, certainly well enough for Hannah to leave the house without it falling through. She placed a fitted t-shirt over the top. It wouldn't hide much, but it would give the impression that she had nothing to hide. She casually held her jacket in her hand.

Hannah took one last look around her room. She'd been so pleased when she moved in. She'd been proud of having two double beds, and her own bathroom with its high-quality fixtures and fittings. She'd thought she deserved it, that it was her due. But now, everywhere she looked, she only saw what was missing. Without Freddie, the room was soulless. His absence highlighted her hubris. She hadn't earned the right to a room like this. Worse, she had been bribed with it, and she'd allowed her pride to blind her to her situation. Now, she was happy to be leaving it behind.

As she stood in front of the mirror, she took a deep breath in, and exhaled, slowly, repeating until her heart rate calmed, and the effects of the adrenaline pumping through her lessened. In and out. In and out. She would only have one shot at this. She had to get it right.

Stepping upstairs, Hannah was glad to see Katie was at the far end of the kitchen. Distance helped her illusion, and all she had to do was to keep herself front-facing. The outline of her passport would be easily visible if she turned, and it would fall if she moved too much. But for now, it remained snugly in place.

Katie held a roller in her hand. She appeared to have washed the walls as well as she could. The blood was lighter, muted, with its spurting pattern less defined. She was starting to re-paint the wall with a sunny yellow colour. It was going to take at least two coats to cover up the evidence of Freddie's slaughter.

Of Freddie himself, there was no indication left that he had ever existed. Hannah noted, with a lump in her throat, that his bowl had been removed as well as his body. Determined to keep on track, she took a deep breath, and plastered a smile on her face.

"Morning Katie, have you really been working all night?" Hannah opened the fridge and took her water bottle from the shelf, placing it on the island before leaning over to take an energy bar from the cupboard. "Still, I can't say I've had any sleep myself. I feel agitated. I couldn't settle."

"Of course, hun," said Katie, placing her roller down and wandering over to the island. Save for the greasiness of her hair, it wasn't possible to tell she'd been working hard all night.

Hannah balanced her running pack on top of the island surface, unzipped it and placed the energy bar inside, on top of her phone.

Look Katie, I'm not hiding anything.

Such demonstrations, she hoped, would convince Katie she was not leaving for good. She took her time zipping it back up, letting Katie reach the other side of the island and get close enough to see inside.

"I'm not surprised you couldn't sleep, it was a really traumatic night, I know. But you seem to have calmed down a little."

"I have." Hannah nodded to reinforce her words, which were well-rehearsed. "Don't get me wrong, I'm a long way from being happy about it all, but I will make amends with Emily. I appreciate I didn't act as well as I could have done either. So, yeah, I am starting to work through it, but it's going to take some more time, though."

"Sure, sure," said Katie, eyeing her closely. "Off out?"

"Yeah, I need to run. I need to get my first run without Freddie behind me, and I need to feel better than I currently do. Besides, I always run first thing in the morning."

"Bit early, isn't it? Not even six o'clock yet." Katie leant on the island as if trying to close the distance between them. "It's still dark out."

"It'll be dark for hours yet." Hannah hoped she sounded breezy. She twisted her jacket and flung it around her shoulders, looking as casual as possible, while loosely tying the arms together. It was the best she could do, and she hoped it would work. It was time to try leaving.

"It's the time of year, you have to be willing to run in the dark when it's winter." Hannah picked up her water bottle and wandered towards the door, taking care not to appear to rush. Her back was covered by both the jacket and its hood, but she was still tense, sure the outline of her passport would show through the thin clothing.

"I'll see you in a couple of hours for some breakfast." Hannah found it much easier to lie when she wasn't face-to-face with Katie, and she was sure her tone gave nothing away.

She reached to open the door, resisting the temptation to yank it open and dash out.

"Hannah, haven't you forgotten something?"

She halted and exhaled, torn between her desire to flee, and her willingness to fight if she had to. She admitted to herself, if Katie forced her to hit her then she would take great pleasure in doing so.

Inhaling, Hannah pivoted back towards Katie. She was holding out a small package, but not coming any closer to her.

"Your caffeine pills. Don't you normally take these before you run?"

Hannah's heart was beating fast enough, she didn't need any further stimulation. She sensed a trap, felt herself being drawn away from the door and back into the kitchen, away from her goal. Her instinct was to run, but her ruse required her to be calm.

Katie smiled as Hannah took the pills from her, palmed two and dry-swallowed them.

"Thanks," she said, opening her water bottle and drinking from it as she turned again. "I'd have regretted that after a few miles."

She was back at the door before Katie could answer, fearful that she'd find something else to stop her as she was on the brink of being free. Hannah twisted the handle, but the door wouldn't open. She shook it gently, trying not to let her rising panic show, before she shook it a little harder, tears threatening to spring.

"You've forgotten about the new bolt, Hannah. And after we had it fitted to protect you, as well."

Hannah's eyes dropped to the shiny black bolt across the bottom of the door. She bent gingerly, eager not to let the passport slip or show, while wanting to look as natural as possible. She was now convinced that this was all a rouse. There would always be some reason for delaying her, for preventing her from leaving.

The bolt slipped back soundlessly, and with a last twist, the door opened, and Hannah stepped out into the quiet street.

"Bye," she said, and closed the door behind her. She jogged up the street, taking her normal route towards the park. She didn't look back.

She ran away from Emily, from the troupe, and from the life she had built there. Hannah didn't yet know what sort of life she was running towards but, as she picked up her pace, she was sure she was running away from the worst mistake she had ever made.

Chapter Twenty-Seven

Hannah ran, and as she ran, she felt better. She felt free.

Her mind was racing as fast as her legs were. She had been so sure that Katie was teasing her that she had sprinted as soon as she was out of sight of the house, certain she'd be followed and hauled home. Now, she wasn't sure whether Katie had known but let her go or had been convinced by her story. But then, Hannah realised, it didn't matter to her anymore. She was running free.

She held her passport in one hand and her water bottle in the other, pounding them up and down as she circled through Hyde Park. It was busy with early morning dog walkers, the sight of which brought bile back into Hannah's throat. So, she avoided the main strip, and headed off into the minor paths which criss-crossed the park. Contrary to everyone else, she felt safer in the dark than under the streetlights.

She did not know whether Emily would try to find her. Her thoughts were erratic, recalling every detail of her previous escapes from families. The ways she had been found, the successes she'd had, the challenges that she knew lay ahead of her. She left the park, choosing side-streets to avoid the crush of office workers walking their commute, making it easier to see if she was being followed. She threw her mobile phone into a bin, in case tracking software had been added without her knowledge. She would not be in touch with them again, not even Farooq. She couldn't trust any of them to support her rather than Emily. In that world she was no one without Emily's good favour, and so, she was on her own.

She only had the start of a plan, so far. She knew where she was going, but not what reception awaited her when she arrived. It was always a painful process to renew herself, to accept that her attempts to bond with a family had failed. But she was experienced at doing so, and knew she could mask any emotions which might prove unhelpful to her task. She was not sure what reason she was going to give for her sudden change of heart, but she wouldn't tell anyone the truth. It was too shameful to admit to.

When Carly and Robert had been her family, she hadn't needed to re-model herself after their rejection of her. It was her that had rejected them. It had only been a few hours since Carly had begged her to come home. How swiftly Hannah's fortunes had changed. Then, she had been sure of her place in Emily's world, was confident about her future. So much so that she had dismissed Carly's fears and tears, and left her behind with barely a second thought. Now, she ran, her life in tatters, hoping there would be a role for her, something she could salvage. There was nowhere else for her to go.

Hannah tried to picture the scene, to prepare herself, to practice what she was going to say. Her rehearsals floundered because she struggled to know how to begin. She couldn't tell them about Freddie. She couldn't bring herself to admit that they had been right all along. Better to find a more positive approach, something that convinced them she had returned because she wanted to, rather than because she didn't have any other options.

She could say she had returned because Carly had convinced her to come home. If Carly remained as desperate as she was the night before then she would want to believe it was true. Hannah could be vague as to the circumstances of her leaving Emily's, and tell Carly she had chosen her after all. She could even say she had fallen out with Emily over it, make use of Carly's obvious jealousy. It could work as a big gesture.

What gave Hannah pause for thought was remembering the news Carly had given her. Robert was leaving London. When Hannah thought about Robert, her heart swelled and her optimism rose, whereas thoughts of Carly were tinged with grey despair. Robert had carved a new path for himself, one without them both, and had experienced his first tastes of success. There would be more, she was sure. Carly, however, was destined to stay where she was.

Hannah's pace slowed as she came nearer to Camden Town. The quality of the footpaths was poorer, with repeated patch-ups from underground works and the potholes badly filled. There were more people living rough on the street here – they weren't tolerated in Kensington – and she gave them a wide berth as they slept higgledy-piggledy across the pavement. The shops had their shutters pulled down. The place looked neglected and dirty. Unsafe.

She pushed her passport into her waistband behind her running pack and pulled her jacket down, covering it as best she could. Her passport was more valuable than the money she carried, but she didn't want either to be stolen from her. It felt a long time since she had run through streets like these. She had forgotten how downtrodden some parts of London were. Having experienced the fancier parts of the city, she could not imagine settling back into its seedier side. Hannah was certain she would leave London if she could.

Hannah had no intention of talking Robert out of leaving London, as Carly had suggested. She meant to go with him. They would leave London together and start somewhere new. And leaving Carly behind would mean they could leave that ridiculous pact behind. Without her, maybe they would have a chance to be happy together.

She slowed to a walk, turning off the main street into a no-through road, terraced houses along each side. There were no rough sleepers here, but there were overflowing bins, and cars parked half on the pavements. Security lights were triggered as she ran past.

The squat was at the end of the street, facing the rest of the road. The turning circle was large, and so was the house. It must have been grand once. Back then, there would have been factories on every street in this part of town, and the workers would have lived alongside the owners. Wealth and poverty side by side. Not like now.

Hannah was nervous but she felt more powerful than she could ever recall feeling before. Something in her had shifted. This renewal would create a version of herself who was more confident and more determined. Someone who knew how much she was valued by those around her. Someone who knew what she wanted, and knew how to get it.

Chapter Twenty-Eight

Hannah was not one to let an opportunity go to waste.

As she stared at the house and contemplated her future, the light from her old room disappeared. The whole house was now in darkness, seemingly peaceful, but then the front door opened. Headlights flashed by Hannah, and a car paused in front of the squat, illuminating the figure in the doorway.

Hannah gasped. She had not dared hope for such a fortuitous event as this.

Robert manoeuvred a large suitcase through the door, carefully closing it behind him. He greeted the taxi driver, who helped him lift it into the boot, the slamming lid echoing around the street in a way the softly closed door had not.

Hannah was in no doubt, he was going to the airport. She had arrived at the very moment he was leaving for his new life. If there had been any doubt left in her mind, this alignment of their fates should convince them both that they were meant to be together.

She could not believe how serendipitous this was. Her plan needed adapting, and she threw herself into making the most of this opportunity.

Sprinting, Hannah shouted, "Robert! Robert, wait!"

Robert looked up over the roof of the taxi, a streetlight casting a shadow over his face so that his expression was lost.

Hannah assumed he'd be shocked to see her, but happily so. She placed her arms on the other side of the roof and panted, exaggerating, trying to catch her breath, while saying, "I'm glad I'm in time. I want to talk to you."

She heard the smile in his voice. "It's good to see you, it really is. But you're not in time, I've got to go. I've a flight to catch. Maybe ring me later?" Robert opened the rear car door as if to reinforce his point.

"No, no. I need to chat with you face to face. I'll come with you." Hannah yanked the other door open and jumped in before Robert could say otherwise. He crouched to look at her but she still couldn't see well enough to read his expression. She put her seat belt on, reinforcing her point in return. "I'll come for the drive and talk to you on the way. I insist."

As Robert got in, and the taxi drove away, Hannah felt pleased with herself. Her new approach to people – being more insistent with them – appeared to be working well so far.

As the taxi navigated the morning rush-hour traffic, Hannah realised this was going to be a little harder than she'd first thought. Robert sat in silence, his face turned away from her, his arms tightly pressed together. He did not appear as happy to see her as she'd thought. She couldn't work out why he was acting so cold towards her.

"So–" she started, but didn't get any further before Robert interrupted.

"I hope you haven't come for another row. I'm tired of fighting with you."

Hannah's memory of their last meeting flooded back. She had slapped him. They had argued because he had tried to warn her about Emily. He had seen how dangerous she was, how bad she was for Hannah, and yet she hadn't listened to him. She hadn't believed him, had thought she knew better, that he was jealous of her new life. She'd paid it so little attention that she hadn't even

238

remembered that she'd done it. Hannah reassured herself that it was the stress of the night's events which was interfering with her recall.

"I haven't, I promise. I've come to apologise." Hannah chose her words with care. "It was awful of me to strike you. You know it's not like me at all. I'm so sorry. I didn't want you to leave without us making up. I couldn't stand it if you thought the worse of me for it."

"Well, thank you, I suppose. I had given up hope that you were ever going to turn up again, let alone apologise. What's changed? Why this morning?"

Thank you Carly!

"Oh, I take it Carly didn't tell you then? She invited me to meet her last night. She said you were leaving. She asked me to get you to stay."

Robert whipped round to look directly at her, causing her to jolt back to her own side of the car. Passing headlights repeatedly flashed across his stern features. He held her gaze as he responded, "I find that hard to believe. Why would she do such a thing?"

"I'll show you her messages." Hannah dropped her eyes and fiddled with her bag, hoping that would be enough. "She said you were going to start somewhere new, make a film to show how you do it. How else would I have known to come today?"

"Yes, okay, I believe you, of course I do. But I'm confused as to why she'd think you'd be interested in what I was doing. It's been a long time now since you left us, and you've made your feelings for me perfectly clear."

"That's just it," said Hannah, tense now, knowing it would be easy to overdo it and ruin everything. "Only when I heard you were leaving did I realise how much I was missing you. I haven't slept all night. I came here as soon as I could."

"Hmmm. I don't know, Hannah. It's hard to trust you. Still, I don't want to part on bad terms either."

"Then let's not. Right, that's that settled then. So, tell me, where are you going and what are you going to do when you get there?"

Robert laughed. "Okay, okay. So, I'm flying to Venice. The crew are already out there, they start filming the moment I step off the plane. Nothing else is arranged, I've barely any money to my name, the point is to show how to find your way in the streets of a new city. It's a novel idea, the team is really excited about it."

Hannah nodded along as Robert enthused about his forthcoming trip. Her mind was whirling, planning, rehearsing. She smiled in the right places, making the occasional animated noise. Robert needed little encouragement to talk about his future, as energised as he was.

"Here we are, that was quick," he said, pausing his chatter as the taxi pulled up at the airport.

Hannah said nothing, knowing how critical this moment was to her plan.

Robert took his time, fetching his suitcase from the boot and paying the driver, generous as ever with his tip.

Hannah came to stand alongside him, allowing other passengers to flow around them on their way along the concourse. She stood closer to him than someone might normally stand.

Finally, unable to delay any longer, he turned towards her.

Hannah took the initiative before he could say anything. "Let's not say goodbye. I'll see you again soon. For now, let's just agree that I'll see you soon, and that when I do, we won't talk of this whole mess ever again. A new start. Promise?"

"Okay. Promise." Robert beamed and Hannah was momentarily stricken by her emotions. She did love him, she truly did, and she was sure he adored her. If he knew what had happened to her, he would understand, he would do the same thing she was about to, she was sure.

Swift, she placed her lips on his, pressing to make her intent clear, but not deepening or prolonging the kiss. She pulled away before he could.

"See you soon." She jogged away along the taxi rank, leaving Robert staring after her.

Chapter Twenty-Nine

Two hours later, Hannah was the last passenger to board. Her seat was at the back and she boarded from the rear of the plane, unseen by all but her nearest fellow fliers. She tightened her seatbelt and tried to relax. She was escaping.

One advantage to sitting at the rear was being the first to be served with drinks. Though it was far too early and only a short flight, Hannah bought two miniature bottles of gin. She deserved it after the twenty-four hours she'd had. She swallowed the first in one gulp, barely watered down with tonic, only then realising how strung out she was. She hadn't eaten since the evening before and, of course, she hadn't eaten much.

Thoughts about food caused Hannah to reflect; which elements of her life with Emily did she want to keep? She poured her second drink while thinking it would be a shame to completely dismiss everything she had learnt. Some of those new behaviours would be crucial as she created a new persona, a new lifestyle. Besides, Hannah had grown fond of her skinnier body, and would not hurry to throw all that hard work away.

"Hannah? What?"

She looked up to see Robert, blocking other passengers, glowering at her and causing the man sitting in the aisle seat to slide backwards as far as he could, trying to keep out of their way.

"Answer me, Hannah. What on earth are you doing here?"

Hannah didn't say anything. Everything rested on her getting this moment right.

243

She downed the second drink, and eased past the man, to his evident relief at being recused from this drama. Hannah moved close to Robert and, ignoring the huffs from other passengers, took hold of his hand.

"I told you I'd see you soon."

"But, but…" Robert dropped his eyes but didn't pull away, which Hannah took as a good sign.

"And you promised me, don't forget."

His head jerked back up. "You tricked me?"

"No, no, that's not true. No, I'm surprising you. I'm coming with you. I love you. I couldn't let you leave me behind."

She squeezed Robert's hand, giving him a moment to say he loved her as well. It was ruined by a woman pushing her way past them both, her blonde hair whipping their faces as she flew past, muttering about the selfishness of young people. Hannah tried again.

"I've realised we belong together, so I had to do something to show you how serious I am. I've left everything behind to come and join you. I love you."

Rather than give him the time to not reply, she kissed him, a little rougher than she'd intended. As she felt him respond, the knot in her stomach started to unwind.

Robert sighed. "I suppose this is what people in love do, isn't it? Make grand gestures. Hard to say no, isn't it?"

It wasn't the declaration of undying love Hannah had hoped for, but then, there was time yet. She was sure that with her newly acquired skills, that would soon change.

"Excellent!" Hannah gripped Robert in a hug, as an announcement asked passengers to prepare for their arrival in Venice.

"I'd better get back to my seat," Robert said as he eased away from her.

Hannah gripped his wrist, using her other hand to stroke the side of his face, looking deep into his eyes as she traced his jawline and brushed a finger over his lips, before letting him go and moving back to her seat as elegantly as she could.

As she sat, she saw Robert was still standing there, staring at her.

Yes, I've learnt a few things from Emily which are going to prove useful.

As Robert hustled away and the plane was prepared for landing, Hannah closed her eyes and laid back her head. She imagined herself gliding in a gondola, sunshine caressing her bare skin, Robert gazing adoringly at her. The hole in her heart was not going to heal quickly, but she had a new start to look forward to, a life that was hers to make a success of. A life in Venice, the most romantic city in the world.

She was sure Robert would see things her way soon. After all, she was statuesque.

About Ada Rossi

Ada Rossi is a UK based author with Italian heritage, writing from her home in the north of England while admiring her views of the countryside where her partner farms. She is experimental in her writing, creating contemporary and historical fiction which is sometimes thought provoking, sometimes heart wrenching, and always absorbing. When she's not writing she is sharing her love of books, cats and coffee on social media.

Other BDP books by Ada Rossi

Terrifying Love - A Halloween Anthology
Beautiful Tragedy - A Halloween Anthology
The Condemned Oak Tree
Golden Tattoo - A Halloween Anthology

CPSIA information can be obtained
at www.ICGtesting.com
Printed in the USA
LVHW091538100922
728014LV00015B/502